My Treasury of Five-Minute TALES

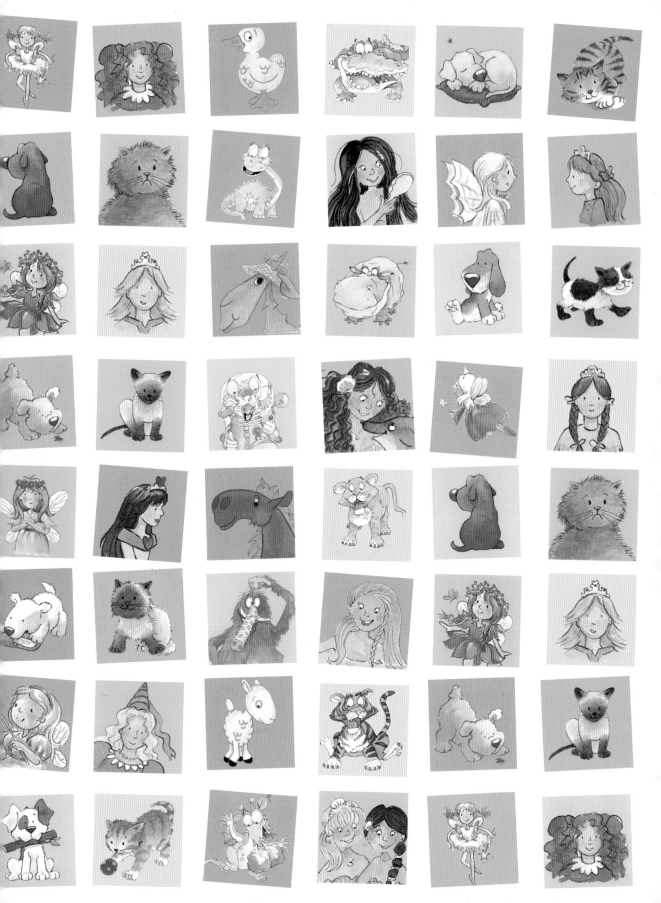

This book belongs to

Katy - from Gran + Grande.
Christmas
2004

My Treasury of Five-Minute TALES

p

CONTENTS

— Old —
EVEREST

Everest was one of the biggest horses in the world. He was also one of the strongest. When he was young, and already twice as big as other horses, he pulled the heavy cart filled with peas or potatoes, cabbages or corn, and everything grown on the farm. He took the vegetables from the farm down to the market, and he brought things from the market back to the farm. He pulled the huge machine that cut the wheat to make flour. He pulled the big plough that dug the soil, so the farmer could plant the seed that grew into wheat that made the flour…

...that Everest took to market. He did everything!

Everest was the best...but that was ages ago.

"So why don't you do everything now?" asked Puff the pig.

"The farmer thinks I'm too old," said Everest, sadly. "He is only trying to be kind. He thinks I need a rest."

Jacob the lamb said, "I bet you are still stronger than anything, Everest! Nothing is as strong as you!" The huge horse lowered his head.

"Well...I am not as strong as I was, little one," smiled Everest. "Anyway, farms don't use horses any more. The farmer uses a tractor instead!"

The big old horse had lots of time to think about when he was young and still worked on the farm. He spent most of the time now in his favourite meadow nibbling grass, and, when he grew bored with that, chasing rabbits or chickens, or biting large chunks out of the hedge. But if Parsnip the sheep, Waddle the goose, or Scratchitt the cat were in his field, he would tell them his stories. Sometimes he told the same stories again without realising, but no one really minded.

But Everest still thought about the tractor. It wasn't the tractor's fault. He just wanted to work.

"Can this tractor pull the cart better than you?" asked Parsnip the sheep.

"No," said Everest.

"Can the tractor pull the plough better than you?" asked Waddle the goose.

"No," said Everest.

"Can the tractor cut the wheat better than you?" asked Scratchitt the cat.

"No," said Everest.

"So why did the farmer buy the tractor?" Puff the pig wanted to know. Everest lowered his huge head and sighed.

"He liked the colour," said Everest.

Then one day the farmer said to Everest, "I have a problem with that tractor of mine. It won't start! I would ask you to help, Everest, but I suppose you are enjoying your rest." Everest shook his head from side to side.

"Even so," said the farmer, "I need to plough the field and the plough won't fit a horse, just the tractor! I don't know what to do."

Everest nudged the farmer gently over to the barn where the tractor was kept. His reins and harness were there too. The puzzled farmer picked up an old rope and hooked it on the front of the tractor. Then, as easily as anything, Everest pulled the tractor out. Then he pulled the plough up behind the tractor.

"You mean you can pull both together?" said the farmer. Everest nodded his head up and down. The farmer was amazed! So the farmer hooked the plough to the tractor. Then he hooked the tractor to the horse. And Everest pulled the tractor and the tractor pulled the plough.

Together they ploughed the field in the fastest time ever.

Everest was still the biggest and the strongest... and now the happiest horse in the whole world.

The CHICKLINGS

Duck and Hen both laid some eggs. They were very proud mothers. They would sit with silly smiles on their faces, fondly waiting for their eggs to hatch.

"Duck," said Hen, "let us put the eggs side by side, and see whose eggs are the most beautiful."

"If you like," said Duck, "but I already know mine are."

"Ha!" said Hen. "Wait until you have seen mine!"

Duck carried her eggs carefully, one by one, to a spot where there was soft hay on the ground. Hen carried her eggs over to the same spot and gently set them down beside Duck's. Duck picked up the first egg from her side.

"Look at this one! This egg is so smooth!" she said. They both looked at how smooth the egg was. Hen picked up an egg too.

"This one is smooth as well…and it is so round! Look at the lovely shape of this egg." They both looked at the shape of the egg. They put back those two eggs and picked up two others.

Duck said, "This one is smooth and shapely, and has beautiful freckles…"

By the time the last one was picked up and put back, the eggs were all mixed up together!

Hen said, "I am fatter than you, so my eggs must be the largest ones." So Duck picked out the smallest eggs and put them back in her nest. Hen picked out the largest eggs and took them back to hers. Then they sat on them until the eggs hatched and out popped fluffy ducklings and chicks.

One day Duck and Hen met with their babies.

"Now!" said Duck proudly. "Aren't these the handsomest ducklings you ever saw?"

"They are quite handsome," replied Hen, "but don't you think these are the most beautiful chicks in the whole world?"

"They are quite beautiful," replied Duck.

The next day, Duck taught her ducklings how to be ducklings.

"Walk behind me, one behind the other!" she told them. "We are going to the pond for swimming lessons." But the ducklings just couldn't walk one behind the other. They ran circles around Duck. They ran over her and under her, until Duck became quite dizzy watching them scoot about. When they reached the pond, the ducklings dipped their feet in the water, shook their heads and refused to go in.

Hen was teaching her chicks how to be chicks. She taught them to scratch and hop backwards to make the worms pop up out of the ground. But the chicks couldn't do it! They fell on their faces instead. She taught them to run all over the farm and look for their own food. They just followed her everywhere in a long line.

When Hen's back was turned, the chicks would cram into the dog's drinking bowl and would not come out! Josh the dog was lying next to his bowl. He opened one eye but didn't seem to mind. He would rather drink from the puddles anyway.

Duck and Hen sighed and sat down together to talk. They knew by now that they had each taken the wrong eggs. The ducklings were chicks, and the chicks were ducklings.

"Never mind," said Hen. "Let's just call them chicklings, and we will always be right."

"One thing we have found out," said Duck. "is that the chicklings are all beautiful. We would not have mixed them up, otherwise." Hen agreed, and they sat all afternoon, happily watching their chicklings play.

The ducklings played in the dog's bowl...

And the chicks played on the dog!

AUNTY
and the flowers

Every year on the farm, the animals had a competition. Everyone liked to join in the fun, and there was a prize for the winner. The prize could be for anything. One year, it was for growing the best purple vegetables. Once it was for having the knobbliest knees. (Gladys the duck won that,

of course.) Once it was for the animal who could spell 'chrysanthemum'. The prize was not won at all that time...no one in the world can spell chrysanthemum! This year they decided the prize would be for the best display of flowers. But who would choose the winner? Most of the animals had already been judges in other years. Some of them had been judges more than once.

If Nelly the hen were the judge, she would make herself the winner. She always did.

Bramble the sheep caught her wool on everything. She pulled the tables and chairs down behind her wherever she went.

Blink the pig covered everything in mud.

Rambo the big horse couldn't even get into the tent!

But Aunty the goat wanted the job. She told the others how much she liked flowers. So why not? Aunty had never been a judge before and so she was chosen.

The big day came. Everyone had been busy for days. The tent was full of flowers, full of colour and light. There were no brown leaves on the flowers. There were no creepy-crawlies on the leaves. There was just a lovely smell of roses, and the animals waiting excitedly for the doors to open. Perfect!

The judge, Aunty the goat, went first. She looked very important. Then all the rest came in, one at a time. Last was Rambo, the big horse, who just poked in his head. Aunty was taken to the first display by Bramble the sheep.

"So I just choose which flowers I like best?" Aunty asked.

"Yes, we walk along the table, and whichever display you think is best wins the prize. This is Blink's display. She has spent all morning getting it just right."

"It's called 'Daisies and Dandelions'," said Blink proudly. The flowers were white and yellow and looked very pretty in a bright blue mug. Aunty looked at them carefully. She sniffed them. And then she ate them.

The others were so surprised, that they couldn't speak! They just stared as Aunty went to the next one, 'Buttercups and Roses'. She ate them too!

The goat tilted her head back, half closed her eyes in a very thoughtful sort of way, and compared 'Buttercups and Roses' with 'Daisies and Dandelions'.

Moving along the line, she ate 'Cowslips and Honeysuckle'. Then she ate 'Poppies and Krezanthasums... Crissansathums... Chrismasathumbs... Poppies and another flower we can't spell!' Aunty wrinkled up her nose.

"Bit sour, that," she said. She turned at last and saw all the others looking at her with their mouths open. She looked from one to the other, red poppies drooping from the sides of her mouth.

"What?" she said, puzzled. "What!"

Rambo said gently, "You were supposed to judge how pretty the flowers are!"

Aunty was amazed.

"Flowers are pretty as well?" she asked.

Everyone burst out laughing. They had to explain it all to Aunty. She thought the whole idea of just looking at flowers was very odd.

There was no time to pick more flowers and start again. Instead, they gave Blink the prize...Aunty had decided that Blink's 'Daisies and Dandelions' tasted the best!

At the end, the judge is always given a bunch of flowers as a small, 'thank you' gift. Aunty was so pleased...she ate it!

- Cuddly's -
JUMPER

Cuddly Sheep and Stout Pig were going to show the others how to knit. Cuddly Sheep was really good at knitting. But she needed her friend, Stout Pig, to help with the wool. Stout Pig couldn't knit, not even a little bit, but he was very good at spinning the wool for Cuddly to use.

Wool has to be made into yarn before you can knit with it. Yarn is made by twisting it, like string. That is what Stout did. He collected all the loose bits of wool that caught on thorny bushes around the farm and made long, beautiful lengths of yarn out of them. Then

Cuddly used Stout Pig's yarn to knit lots of pretty things. She could knit woolly socks. She could knit woolly hats. She could knit the best woolly jumpers in the world!

Cuddly and Stout sat close to each other. Stout Pig sat with his back against a low hedge and Cuddly sat on the other side. The pig pulled out lengths of wool from a pile under the hedge. He started to spin the wool on his wheel, until it was twisted into yarn and long enough to knit. Then he gave the end to Cuddly.

Cuddly made little loops of the wool and put them on two fat knitting needles. Then she started knitting.

"Knit one, purl one, knit two together," she whispered to herself. Only knitters know what these secret words mean. They must be magic words, because they are whispered over and over again.

"Knit one, purl one, knit two together."

The jumper quickly started to take shape. As it grew in size, the animals watching could see it was nearly all white, just like the colour of Cuddly's own

woolly jumper, with little bits in purple, like the berries on the hedge.

"Knit one, purl one, knit two together."

Stout had to work hard on the other side of the hedge to keep up with Cuddly Sheep.

"Knit one, purl one, knit two together…"

Cuddly looked up. "Is it getting late? I'm getting a bit cold," she said. None of the others felt cold.

"You can put my blanket on," said Pebbles the horse. He pulled his blanket over Cuddly's shoulders. But Cuddly got colder. And colder!

"I keep warm in the straw," said Saffron the cow. She covered Cuddly with straw. But the more Cuddly

knitted, the colder she got. And the hotter Stout became. Cuddly was trying to finish the jumper quickly before she froze. The faster she knitted, the faster Stout Pig had to turn the spinning wheel, and he was soon in a sweat!

Then the jumper was finished…and Cuddly was shivering! Her teeth were chattering! Stout Pig flopped over the spinning wheel, trying to get his breath back. He was so hot and tired. Pebbles looked hard at Stout.

"Where did the wool come from that you were spinning?" he asked.

"I used that bundle of wool under the hedge," said Stout. "It was here when I came."

Pebbles' large head followed the wool from the spinning wheel over the hedge. There was only Cuddly there. "Cuddly," said Pebbles '...I think you have been knitting your own wool!"

Cuddly jumped up in surprise. The blanket and the straw fell off. She was bare all around her middle. No wonder she was cold. Her wool was all gone!

"Oh well," said Cuddly Sheep, taking out the needles from her knitting. "Never mind! I have a nice thick new jumper to keep me warm!"

— Clever —
BOOGIE

Boogie was a very clever pig. Most pigs aren't clever. They can't do sums. They can't tie their own shoelaces. Every single day they are given pig food to eat, and they say, "Oink! Oink! Pig food! My favourite!" They don't remember it's always the same.

But Boogie remembered every horrible meal he'd ever had, and was really fed up with pig food. It tasted like minced rubbish! Boogie lived in his own pen. It had a little shelter to keep the rain off, and a small run to play in. In the field outside the pigpen lived a sheep, a horse and a cow. There were trees in the field too, but none near Boogie.

One day, acorns started falling from the biggest tree. The tree was a long way from Boogie, but just a few acorns bounced over and into his pen. Apples began falling from another tree, and one rolled and rolled, until it rolled into Boogie's pen.

Now, usually the only thing inside a pigpen is a pig. They eat everything else! They eat the grass, the roots, worms, stinging nettles, everything! All that is left is a pig in mud! Pigs think anything else in a pen must be food. So Boogie ate the acorns.

You probably know that acorns are really horrible to eat, but Boogie thought they were delicious! Then he ate the apple. He had never eaten anything so good in his life! He wanted all the acorns and apples! They were all around him, but he could not reach them. But he was a clever pig after all. Suddenly he had an idea.

Next to Boogie's pigpen was an old animal shed that had fallen to bits. Bricks and wood were spread about and wavy metal roof panels lay nearby.

Boogie said to the cow, "Will you move that metal roof for me? I'll give you some of my food if you do."

"I have all this grass to eat!" said the cow.

"But that's just plain grass," said Boogie. "This is pig food flavour in lumps!"

"Oh, all right!" said the cow. She pushed the roof under the apple tree.

"There! Is that in the right place?"

"Just move it forward…now turn it towards me… Good!"

Boogie gave the cow some of his pig food. The cow chewed for ages before she realised pig food did not have any actual taste in it. She spat it out.

"Pwah! Tastes like minced rubbish!" she said, and trotted off.

Boogie said to the horse, "Will you move that barrel for me? I'll give you some of my food if you do."

"I have all this grass to eat!" said the horse.

"But yours is green grass," said Boogie. "This is rich brown pig food in lumps!" So the horse moved the barrel where Boogie wanted it and was given the rest of the pig food.

"Yuck!" said the horse, when he tried it. "Do you really eat this rubbish?" And he galloped off too.

Boogie looked at the sheep. The sheep said, "I know – you want me to move something! I'll do it, but please don't give me any pig food!"

The sheep moved the drainpipe to where Boogie wanted it.

When the next apple fell, it rolled down the iron roof into the drainpipe and flew into Boogie's pen!

An acorn bounced off the barrel, and soon there were apples and acorns falling everywhere and bouncing into Boogie's pen.

Boogie dashed around, catching apples and acorns before they could even touch the ground!

And he never had to eat pig food again!

Lizzie and the
TRACTOR

Little Yellow the tractor came to a halt next to Lizzie the cow. The farmer leaned out of the tractor cab.

"Come on Lizzie, get up!" said the farmer. "We have the big farm show in one week. How are you going to win the 'Best Cow' prize if you laze around all day getting plump? You're so lazy!"

"I like lying here!" said Lizzie the cow. "I have all the grass I need right here next to me. I don't even have to get up!"

"You used to be the pride of the show, Lizzie!" wailed the farmer. "Wouldn't you like to be again?"

Lizzie munched on her mouthful and thought about it.

"No!" she said.

The farmer did not know what to do. All his animals won prizes except Lizzie. Perhaps they would know how to make Lizzie fit and lovely again.

He drove Little Yellow around the farm to ask their advice. Gorgeous the pig said, "She is too dull! Paint her pink with brown spots...it always works for me."

Reckless the goat said, "She eats too much grass. Get her to eat newspapers...it always works for me!"

Flash the cockerel said, "Her tail is too small. Stick lots of big bright feathers on her bottom…it always works for me!"

The farmer was disappointed. Those were silly ideas. Then Little Yellow said, "I can make Lizzie into the Best Cow again."

The animals snorted with laughter. How could a tractor do anything they could not? But the farmer just said, "Please do everything you can, Little Yellow!"

So Little Yellow bustled around in his barn, humming to himself and trying on all the bits and pieces that a tractor can make use of. First he put on his big bulldozer bucket and went over to Lizzie.

"Please Lizzie, move into the small field."

"Shan't!" said Lizzie, rolling onto her back.

So Little Yellow, to Lizzie's annoyance, scooped her up and took her into the field in the bucket. "It's for your own good," said Little Yellow.

Then Little Yellow put on his plough and, to everyone's amazement, ploughed up the grass in the middle of the field.

Next day, Little Yellow ploughed another strip in the middle of the field, and the day after that too. The ploughed bit was getting bigger and the grassy bit was getting smaller.

"Help!" cried Lizzie. "There is not enough grass left for me to eat! I'm getting thinner!"

Then tractor put on his grass cutter. He mowed all the grass that was left. If Lizzie lay down again she would not get enough to eat.

She had to work hard just to find enough grass. She was smaller now, and the exercise was making her coat glossy.

But the tractor was not finished. He put on his back forks and took Lizzie a bale of hay to eat, but as she rushed to eat it, he drove away, and she had to trot behind to keep up. By the end of the day she was very tired, but fit and healthy too.

By this time, Little Yellow had used nearly every tool he had! The last thing he used was a power spray to wash her down, and…Ta-ra! There stood Lizzie, more beautiful than ever before!

Lizzie went to the show, and of course was declared 'Best Cow'. She had a lovely blue ribbon hung around her neck and the farmer was given a silver cup. All thanks to Little Yellow the tractor!

–Desmond–
GROWS UP

Desmond was the smallest monkey in the group. He couldn't wait to grow up.

"Will you measure me?" Desmond asked his best friend Rodney.

"I only measured you last Monday, and now it's Friday," said Rodney. "You won't have grown in four days!"

"I have," said Desmond stubbornly. "My bones have grown...you'll see."

Rodney took him to the tallest tree in the jungle and made him stand with his back against it. Then he made a mark on the trunk at the top of Desmond's head. It was in the same place as the last mark.

"See," he said, "you are still the same size."

"Botheration!" said Desmond.

One thing Desmond really wanted to do was collect coconuts. All the big monkeys collected coconuts. The small monkeys had to do the washing up! It wasn't fair.

Later he spoke to his friend Bubbles.

"Watch the top of my head," he said to her.

"Whatever for, Dethmond?" said Bubbles. She always called him Dethmond.

"Just watch," said Desmond.

So Bubbles watched the top of his head.

"Well?" asked Desmond.

"Well what?" replied Bubbles.

"Am I growing? Can you see me growing?"

"No, of course not!" she said.

"I knew it!" said Desmond.

"I knew it! I'm never going

to grow."

"Dethmond," said

Bubbles, "you say this every

single day. You will grow!

Honestly you will."

But Desmond was not

so sure.

"What can I do to get

taller?" he asked Rodney.

"Wait!" said Rodney. So

Desmond stood next to

Rodney...and waited.

And waited...and waited...and waited!

"You won't grow that fast!" laughed Rodney. He looked down at his friend. "It will be ages before you grow up."

But Desmond didn't have ages. He wanted to collect coconuts...NOW! He tried to stretch. He asked all his friends to pull on his arms and legs. He asked them to squeeze him so that he would get thinner and taller. He hung from the branches of trees by his toes. But nothing worked!

Every day he watched the other monkeys climb the tall palm trees. Every day he watched as they picked the coconuts and dropped them to the ground.

One day there was a competition to see who could collect the most coconuts. Rodney was the favourite to win. He climbed to the top and wriggled through the palm leaves, and then...oh dear...he got stuck! He made a face as only monkeys can!

"Help!" he called, "I can't move."

One of the other big monkeys went up to try and help, but he was too big to get through the leaves.

"Let me try," begged Desmond.

"If you like," they said grudgingly.

Desmond hurtled up the trunk. At the top he was small enough to reach his friend and help him to get free. Then he picked six or seven coconuts and dropped them to the ground.

When they climbed down the other monkeys crowded round to pat Desmond on the back.

Desmond was as proud as could be.

"Wow!" said Bubbles. "No one has ever, ever climbed a tree that fast before."

"Maybe you are all too big!" said Desmond happily. "Perhaps I won't be in such a hurry to grow up after all!"

After that he didn't worry so much about being small, especially after he collected more coconuts than anyone else, and won the competition!

–The Smiley– CROCODILE

Open-wide was the friendliest crocodile for miles around. While all the grumpy crocodiles were snapping and snarling and being very cross, Open-wide grinned at everyone. He had a very, very big smile.

"You smile too much," the others told him.

"Be fierce...like a real crocodile!"

"I'll try," said Open-wide, and he put on a scowly face.

It lasted two seconds and then the smile came back again.

"How was that?" he asked.

"Hopeless!" the others said. It was no good, he couldn't be grumpy if he tried.

One day, some hippos came to the river. They were very large and there were a lot of them. They waded into the part of the river that the crocodiles liked the best. They splashed and shouted, they dipped and dived, they made a lot of waves and a lot of noise. They were having a really good time.

Open-wide liked watching them having fun. He liked it when they sank to the bottom and then came up very slowly making lots of ripples. He liked it

when they had a contest to see who could make the biggest splash. He liked it when they blew fountains of water up into the air. The grumpy crocodiles didn't like it one little bit!

"We'll soon get rid of them," they said.

Open-wide saw a baby hippo playing in the water. His name was Sausage.

"I bet you can't do this!" said Sausage to Open-wide, and he blew a million bubbles so that they floated in a cloud across the top of the water.

"I bet I can," said Open-wide. And he did... through his nose!

"What about this?" said Sausage, and he turned on his back and sank below the surface. Open-wide did the same, and then he swam very fast to the opposite bank of the river. They played like this all day...and every day after that! Open-wide had never had such a good time.

The grumpy crocodiles were very fed up. They got together to think of ways of getting rid of the hippos. First they tried to look fierce by showing lots of teeth. The hippos just smiled...and showed even bigger teeth!

Then the grumpy crocodiles tried being rude. "Scram!" they shouted...and when that didn't work, "Smelly old hippos!" The hippos thought it was a joke.

Next they charged the hippos while they were swimming. The hippos calmly sank to the bottom of the river where it was too deep for the crocodiles.

The crocodiles didn't know what else to do. Open-wide had an idea!

"Why don't I just smile at them and ask them nicely if they will move?" he said.

"Pooh!" said the crocodiles. "Fat lot of good that will do!"

Open-wide didn't give up. "Please?"

"Oh, go on then," said the grumpy crocodiles,

"but it won't work, you'll see."

But it did! The hippos liked Open-wide. He had a big smile just like them. They listened politely when he explained that the crocodiles didn't really like fun. They would rather be on their own and grumpy.

"We'll move further down the river if you will still come and play with Sausage," they said.

And that's what happened. The crocodiles were amazed! They didn't say anything to Open-wide, but secretly they wondered if smiling *was* better than scowling after all!

-Leo Makes-
A FRIEND

Leo was quite a shy lion. His mum and dad and brothers and sisters were all much bolder. Sometimes he was sad because he didn't have any friends of his own.

"Mum," he said one day, "why will no one play with me?"

"Because other animals think you're frightening," said Mum.

"Pooh," said Leo, "why would anyone be frightened of me?"

"Because you're a lion," said Mum.

It was a lovely day. Leo felt sure he would make a new friend today.

He came to some trees where a group of small monkeys were playing. When the monkeys saw Leo they scampered to the top of the tallest trees.

"Hello," called out Leo.

There was no answer. He could see lots of eyes staring down at him.

"Hello," he called again. "Won't you come down and play with me?"

There was silence. Then one of the monkeys blew a loud raspberry.

"Go away," he said rudely, "we don't like lions!"

"Why not?" asked Leo, giving him a big smile.

"Your teeth are too big," said the monkey, and giggled noisily.

Leo walked on until he came to a deep pool where a hippopotamus and her baby were bathing. Leo watched them playing in the water.

"Hi!" called out Leo. "Can I come in the water with you?"

"No!" said Mummy Hippo.

"But I'd like to play," said Leo.

"So would I!" said Baby Hippo.

"No, you wouldn't," said Mummy Hippo firmly. "You don't play with lions."

"Why not?" asked Baby.

"Because they might eat you!" said Mummy.

"Oh dear," said Baby Hippo.

Puzzled, Leo walked on. He came to an ostrich with its head buried in the sand.

"What are you doing?" asked Leo in surprise.

"Hiding from you!" said the ostrich gruffly.

"But I can still see you!" said Leo.

"But I can't see you!" said the ostrich.

Leo stuck his head in the sand. It felt awful. Sand got in his eyes and in his mouth.

"It feels horrible," he said, spitting sand everywhere.

"Come and play with me instead," said Leo.

"Not likely," said the ostrich. "I don't play with lions, they roar!"

Leo walked on. He saw a snake sunbathing on a rock. He touched the snake gently with his paw.

"Play with me," he said.

"Ouch!" said the snake. "Your claws are too sharp."

Feeling very fed up, Leo sat down under a tree to eat his picnic.

He was all alone. There was no one else in sight.

"I shall just have to get used to playing by myself," he thought.

Suddenly, he heard a small voice say, "Hello!"

Leo looked round. He could see a pair of yellow eyes peeping at him from behind a tree.

"You won't want to play with me," said Leo grumpily, "I've got a loud roar!"

"So have I," said the voice.

"And I've got sharp claws," said Leo.

"So have I," said the voice again.

"And big teeth," said Leo.

"I've got big teeth, too," said the voice.

"What are you?" asked Leo, interested now.

"I'm a lion, of course!"

And into the clearing walked another little lion.

"I'm a lion, too," said Leo, grinning. "Would you like to share my picnic?"

"Yes, please!" said the other lion. They ate the picnic and played for the rest of the afternoon.

"I like being a lion," said Leo happily. He had made a friend at last!

-Grandma- ELEPHANT'S -Birthday-

"Boris," said his parents, "it's a special day today. Can you remember why?" They say elephants never forget, but Boris never *remembered*. He wrinkled his forehead and thought very hard.

"Do I start school today?" he said.

"No," said Dad, shaking his head.

"Is it my birthday?" asked Boris.

"Getting closer," said Mum. "It's Grandma Elephant's birthday! I want you to take her this basket of fruit. Can you remember where she lives?"

"Yes," nodded Boris. Mum gave him the basket of fruit and watched him leave.

Boris walked through the forest. It was very quiet and shady.

"Boo!" shouted a voice suddenly. Boris looked round and saw a very strange animal. It looked like a mouse with wings.

"Do I know you?" asked Boris

"I'm Fruit Bat, ninny," said the fruit bat.

"What do fruit bats do?" asked Boris.

"Eat fruit, of course," said Fruit Bat. "Where are you off to?"

"It's Grandma Elephant's birthday, but I can't remember how to get to her house," said Boris.

"If I tell you, will you give me some fruit?" asked the bat.

Boris nodded.

"That's the path over there," pointed the bat. And he took an apple from Boris's basket.

The path was very narrow. Right in the middle, blocking the way, was a huge gorilla.

"Where do you think you're going?" asked Gorilla.

"I'm taking this basket of fruit to Grandma," said Boris bravely. "It's her birthday."

"Don't you remember who I am?" asked Gorilla.

"Err...you're Crocodile," said Boris.

"No," said Gorilla. "Try again!"

"You're Rhinoceros," Boris tried again.

"If you can't remember who I am," said Gorilla, "you'll have to pay a forfeit."

"What's a forfeit?" Boris asked.

"Something you give me if you get the wrong answer!" said Gorilla. Boris couldn't remember so Gorilla took two bananas and let Boris pass.

Reaching a crossroads, Boris didn't know which path to take.

"Take the left path," said a voice high above him. Looking up, Boris saw Giraffe with his head sticking out of the top of a tree.

"How can you be sure?" asked Boris.

"Are you going to Grandma Elephant's?" asked Giraffe.

"Yes," said Boris.

"I can see her house from up here," said Giraffe.

"Thank you," said Boris. "Have some fruit!"

"That's very kind of you," said Giraffe. He lowered his head and took a pear from the basket.

When Boris arrived at Grandma's house, all that was left in the basket was one juicy plum! What would Grandma say? Would she be cross? He needn't have worried. Grandma hugged him and took him into the kitchen.

There, sitting round the table, were Fruit Bat, Gorilla and Giraffe, all wearing party hats.

In the middle of the table was a big birthday cake, a large

wobbly red jelly, and *all* the fruit they had taken from Boris's basket.

"How sweet of you to arrange a surprise party for me, Boris," said Grandma, hugging him again. They had a lovely time. They played 'Pass the Parcel'. They played 'Hunt the Thimble'. They sang 'Happy Birthday Grandma Elephant'. Grandma said it was the nicest birthday she could remember.

Boris couldn't even remember the way home. So when the party was over his friends took him all the way back. Mum was so pleased to see him.

"Aren't you going to introduce me to your friends?" she asked.

"This is Bat Fruit, Crocodile and Giraffe," said Boris.

Everybody laughed. Silly Boris...what a memory!

COPYCAT
—MAX—

Max was a little tiger with a bad habit. He was a terrible copycat! He copied everyone and everything. When the parrot said, "Pretty Polly, Pretty Polly!" Max repeated it. "Pretty Polly, Pretty Polly!" Then, when the parrot got cross and said, "Shut up, Max, shut up Max," he repeated that as well. It was very annoying.

One day, he set off to explore.

"I shall copy everything I see," he said to himself. And that's when the trouble really started!

First, he saw a bat hanging upside down on the branch of a tree. It was trying to get to sleep.

"I shall go to sleep like that, too," said Max.

"You can't," said the bat. "Only bats sleep like this."

"Hmmm!" said Max, thoughtfully. And he climbed up to the nearest branch, hooked his feet over it and hung upside down.

"Goodnight," he said and shut his eyes.

The next thing he knew he had landed with a crash on the ground.

"I told you!" said the bat. Max picked himself up.

Next, he met a stork standing on one leg.

"Why are you doing that?" asked Max.

"Because it's comfortable," said the stork.

"How long can you do it for?" asked Max.

"For ages!" said the stork. "Only birds can stand like this."

"Hmmm!" said Max, and lifted up one leg.

"Now lift up two more," said the stork. Max did, and fell in a heap on the ground.

"Told you!" said the stork. Max picked himself up.

Exploring further, he met a brown chameleon sitting on a green leaf. The amazing thing about chameleons is that they can change colour when they want to. The chameleon saw Max and changed his colour to green, like the leaf! Max could no longer see him.

"Where have you gone?" asked Max, looking everywhere.

"I'm still here," said the chameleon. "Watch this," he added, and he jumped onto a red flower and turned...red!

"Watch this then," said Max, and he lay down on some grass. "Now I'm green," he said.

"No, you're not," said the chameleon. "Only chameleons can change colour."

"Hmmm!" said Max. He rolled over and over in some mud.

"Look," he said, "now I'm brown." Then he rolled in some white feathers. The feathers stuck to the mud.

"Look," he said, "now I'm all white!"

"It won't last," said the chameleon.

Max decided to set off for home. He passed the stork still standing on one leg. The stork didn't recognize him. He passed the bat, still hanging upside down. The bat didn't recognize him.

He arrived home late in the evening. His brothers and sisters were playing down by the river. They saw a white figure coming towards them.

"WOOooo!" wailed Max, pretending to be a ghost. "I've come to get you!" The tiger cubs were so scared, they rushed into the river and started to swim to the other side.

"WOOooo!" wailed Max and rushed in after them. Of course, as soon as Max got wet, the mud and feathers disappeared. When the others saw it was only Max they were really cross.

"You frightened us," they told him.

"It was only a joke," said Max.

They only agreed to forgive him if he promised not to copy anything again.

"Oh, all right," said Max. And for the moment, he meant it!

- Custard's -
NEW HOME

Custard the little hippo lived where it was very hot. His home was a cool river that flowed into the sea. This was where he met Sid, the hermit crab. Sid and Custard were best friends.

This was a bit odd because they were as different as could be. Custard was a lot bigger than Sid for a start. Custard thought that being a hermit crab must be really cool. Hermit crabs are funny animals. Instead of having one shell like ordinary crabs, they keep changing from one shell to another.

At the moment Sid had a bright pink, pointed shell. He carried it around with him everywhere he went. Custard thought this was really great. He wanted to carry his own home around with him! Then he wouldn't have to stay out in the hot sun. Hippos don't like getting hot. But there are no shells as big as a hippo. So they have to stay in the river to keep cool.

"Will you help me build my own home?" Custard asked Sid one day.

"Of course I will," said Sid. So they built a house of leaves and tied it to Custard's back. Custard was as pleased as could be. They went for a walk by the river. Sid wore a new blue shell this time. He said it was the latest fashion. They passed a lion that had a bad cold. ATISHOO! The lion sneezed loudly and blew Custard's new house away!

"Bother!" said Custard.

So they built another house, this time of bamboo.

"This won't blow away," said Custard.

But an elephant appeared. And, oh dear! Bamboo is an elephant's favourite food.

"Yummy!" said the elephant. "Thanks for bringing me my breakfast!" And he stuffed Custard's house into his mouth!

"That was my new home," said Custard crossly.

"Oops! Sorry," said the elephant.

Sid was looking for a new home for himself. The blue one was getting too small. He thought a yellow one would be nice. A large bird flying lazily overhead spotted Sid without his shell.

"Ah, crab lunch!" it said, and, swooping low, it grabbed Sid in its claws. Sid wriggled and freed himself. He dropped to the ground with a thump.

"Ouch!" he said. Before he could move, the bird tried to grab him again. Custard rushed to help, but was too big and slow. Looking round, he spotted a deckchair, a sunshade and a bucket and spade.

"Quick," he called to Sid, "over here!" Sid dived under the bucket. Just in time! The bird squawked angrily. Custard waved the spade in a big arc over his head, and the bird flew away. Then he wriggled his bottom into the stripy deck chair, and settled down under the shade of the green umbrella. It felt nice and cool.

If only his head and legs didn't stick out in front. He wriggled a bit more trying to get comfortable.

"How do you like your new bucket house?" he asked Sid.

"A bit roomy," answered Sid in a muffled voice. "How's your deck chair?"

"A bit tight," answered Custard.

There was silence for a while, then Custard said, "Sid, I've been thinking."

"Have you, Custard?"

"Yes, I've been thinking that I'll just keep cool in the river like I did before."

"And I think I'll look for another shell," said Sid.

So the two friends wandered back down to the river, happy to be going home together.

– A Perfect –
PUPPY

Polly had wanted a puppy for a long time, so when Mummy and Daddy said yes, she couldn't wait to get to the pet shop.

At the pet shop, Polly inspected the puppies one by one. She wanted to be sure that she chose the right one. After all, her puppy had to be perfect.

"That one's too big," said
Polly, pointing to a Great Dane.
"And that one's too small." She
pointed to a tiny Chihuahua.

"How about this one?" said
Mummy, stroking an Afghan
hound.

"Too hairy."
"Well, how
about this boxer?"

said Daddy, tickling its pink
tummy.

"Not hairy enough."

"This one's nice," said the
shopkeeper, patting a poodle.

"Too curly," Polly declared.

Another puppy was too noisy. And two more were too quiet. Before long, there weren't many puppies left. Polly was about to give up, when something soft rubbed against her leg.

"Ah, perfect," she cried, picking up a small bundle of black and white fur.

"Err, what kind of puppy is it?" asked Daddy.

"It's my puppy," sighed Polly.

"It's a mongrel," said the shopkeeper. "I think it's part spaniel and part collie. We're not really sure."

"I don't care what he is," smiled Polly. "He's just perfect. I'm going to call him Danny."

Danny whined as he left the pet shop. And he whined all the way home. But he stopped whining when he saw the cat. Then he started barking instead.

"He'll be okay once he gets used to us," said Mummy. Polly hoped she was right.

In the afternoon, they took Danny for a walk in the park. Polly took some bread to feed to the ducks. But as soon as Danny saw the ducks he started to bark. Then he began to chase them. He didn't stop until the last duck had flown away.

Polly was so upset that Daddy bought her an ice-cream to cheer her up.

"He's just a puppy. He's got a lot to learn," explained Daddy. But Polly wasn't listening. Danny had jumped up and stolen her ice-cream. Polly was beginning to wonder if she'd chosen the right puppy.

When they got home, Polly decided to show Danny her toys. She was introducing all her dolls and cuddly toys, when Danny pounced on her favourite teddy.

"He's got Mr Fluffy," cried Polly, as Danny raced from the room into the garden. When he came back, Mr Fluffy was gone.

Polly was furious. She waved an angry finger at Danny. "You're not a perfect puppy," she said. "I don't think you'll ever learn."

Poor Danny, he hung his head and slunk away under the table and wouldn't come out all evening.

The next morning, Polly was woken up by something wet pressed against her cheek. She opened her eyes to see what it was. It was Danny, wagging his tail. And in his mouth was Mr Fluffy! Danny dropped Mr Fluffy on the floor for Polly to pick up.

"Good boy, Danny," laughed Polly, tickling his ears. "You are a perfect puppy, after all!"

– Monty the –
MONGREL

Monty was a very curious puppy. He liked nothing better than exploring the garden. "Don't go far," Mummy would say. But Monty wasn't worried about getting lost. He was a very good explorer.

One day, a big lorry pulled up outside the house where Monty lived. Two men began carrying things out of the house. One of them said something about moving, but Monty was just a puppy and didn't know what that meant.

One of the men left the gate open so, when no one was looking, Monty crept out.

Monty had a wonderful time sniffing around other people's gardens. He found lots of yummy things to eat. And some really lovely things to roll in.

After a while, Monty began to feel tired. He was such a good explorer that he sniffed his way home without any trouble.

But when he got there, he couldn't believe his eyes. Everyone, including Mummy and all his brothers and sisters, had gone.

Monty was very surprised but he wasn't too worried. After all, he was a very good explorer. He began sniffing at once.

He soon found himself in the park where he met a group of dogs.

"Who are you?" asked one.

"What kind of dog are you?" asked another.

Monty didn't know who to answer first, so he just stopped sniffing and stared.

"Well, he's not a Poodle," sniffed the first dog, who Monty couldn't help thinking looked like a ball of cotton wool. "He's far too rough."

"He's definitely not a dachshund," said another dog. Monty tried hard not to laugh. He'd never seen anything so long.

"He's certainly not an Old English sheepdog," barked a third dog. "He's just not hairy enough."

"Hmm!" grunted a fourth dog, who had the flattest nose Monty had ever seen. He walked around Monty and stared at him from all sides. Then he stopped and shuddered. "I don't think he's a special kind of dog. I think he's a MONGREL."

"Yes!" barked Monty. He liked the sound of that.

"Well if that's the case," sniffed the cotton wool dog, "he'd better hang out with Tinker."

The long dog nudged Monty towards Tinker. Monty thought Tinker was the most handsome dog he'd ever seen. He had short legs, long ears and a wonderful curly tail. He also had kind eyes.

"Take no notice of them," said Tinker. "They're just trying to help."

Monty gave Tinker a lick, and before long he was telling Tinker about his family.

"Let's walk around the park," said Tinker. "If we follow our noses, we might find your family."

In the park, Monty sniffed the air. He could smell a very familiar smell. Then, he heard a very familiar bark. Suddenly, a huge brown dog bounded out of one of the houses on the other side of the park.

"Run for your lives," yelped the cotton wool dog.

"Help! It's a giant," barked the flat-nosed dog.

"Mummy!" shouted Monty.

"Monty!" barked Mummy. "Thank goodness you're safe."

"Tinker looked after me," said Monty happily.

"So you're a Great Dane puppy," laughed Tinker. "Not a mongrel, after all."

Milly the
GREEDY
—Puppy—

Milly the Labrador puppy just loved eating. She wasn't fussy what she ate, and didn't really mind whom it belonged to.

"You'll get fat," warned Tom, the farm cat. But Milly was too busy chewing a tasty fishbone to take any notice.

One day, Milly was in a particularly greedy mood. Before breakfast she sneaked into the kitchen and ate Tom's biscuits. After a big breakfast of fresh sardines and milk, she took a short break before nibbling her way through the horse's oats. The horse didn't seem to mind.

Then Milly had a quick nap. She felt quite hungry when she woke up, so she ate all the tastiest titbits from the pig's trough. But she made sure she left plenty of room for lunch.

After a light lunch, Milly couldn't help feeling just a bit hungry – so she wolfed down Farmer Jones's meat pie. He'd left it on the window ledge so he obviously didn't want it.

After that, Milly knocked over the dustbin and rifled through the kitchen waste. It was full of the yummiest leftovers. You really wouldn't believe the things that people throw away.

There was just enough time for another nap before nipping into the milking shed for milking

time. Milly always enjoyed lapping up the odd bucketful of fresh milk when Farmer Jones wasn't looking.

Dinner was Milly's favourite meal of the day. It was amazing how fast she could eat a huge bowl of meat and biscuits.

Before going to bed, Milly walked around the yard cleaning up the scraps the hens had left behind. Wasn't she a helpful puppy!

Just as Milly was chewing a particularly tasty bit of bread, she saw something black out of the corner of her eye. It was Tom the farm cat, out for his evening stroll. If there was one thing Milly liked doing best of all, it was eating Tom's dinner when he wasn't looking.

Milly raced across the yard, around the barn and through the cat flap.

"Woof! Woof!" yelped Milly. She was stuck half-way through the cat flap. Greedy Milly had eaten so much food that her tummy was too big to fit through.

"Ha! Ha!" laughed the farm animals, who thought it served Milly right for eating all their food.

"Oh, dear!" smiled Tom when he came back to see what all the noise was about. He caught hold of Milly's legs and tried pulling her out. Then he tried pushing her out. But it was no good, she was stuck.

All the farm animals joined in. They pulled and pulled, until, POP! Out flew Milly.

Poor Milly felt so silly that she never ate anyone else's food again – unless they offered, that is!

Hooray for
PEPPER!

Pepper was a very noisy puppy. He wasn't a bad puppy. He was just so happy that he barked all day long.

"Woof! Woof!" he barked at the cat, and she hissed and ran away.

"Woof! Woof!" he barked at the birds, and they flew up into the tree.

"Woof! Woof!" he barked at the tree, and it waved its branches angrily.

"Woof! Woof!" he barked

at the postman, and he hurried down the garden path.

"Quiet, Pepper!" shouted Jimmy, Pepper's owner. But Pepper just barked back cheerfully.

One day, Pepper had been barking so much that everyone was trying very hard to ignore him.

"Be quiet, Pepper," said Jimmy, as he lay down on the lawn. "I'm going to read my book and I can't concentrate if you keep barking."

Pepper tried his very best not to bark. He tried not to watch the butterflies and bees flitting about the garden. He tried to ignore the bright yellow ball lying on the path. And he tried extra hard not to bark at the birds flying high up in the sky. But everywhere he looked, there were things to bark at, so he decided to stare at the blades of grass on the lawn instead.

As he stared at the grass, Pepper was sure that it began to move. And as he carried on staring, Pepper was sure he could hear a strange slithering sound. He was just about to bark when he remembered Jimmy's words. He carried on staring. Now he could hear a hissing sound. Pepper stared more closely at the grass.

Pepper suddenly started to bark wildly.

"Woof! Woof!" he barked at the grass.

"Sshhh!" groaned Jimmy, as he turned the page of his book.

But Pepper didn't stop. He had spotted something long and slippery slithering across the lawn – something with a long tongue that hissed. Pepper didn't know what it was. But he did know that it didn't look very friendly, and it was heading straight for Jimmy.

"Woof! Woof! WOOF!" barked Pepper, starting to panic. Wasn't anyone going to take any notice of him?

"Quiet, Pepper!" called Jimmy's dad from the house. "How many times have I told you to stop barking?"

But Pepper did not stop barking. He simply barked louder still. Jimmy sat up, and looked around. It wasn't like Pepper to bark quite so much.

"Snake!" yelled Jimmy, pointing at the long slippery snake coming towards him.

Pepper carried on barking as Jimmy's dad raced across the lawn and scooped Jimmy up in his arms. And he carried on barking until a man from the animal rescue centre arrived to take away the snake.

Later, after the man from the animal rescue centre
had taken the snake away, Jimmy patted Pepper and
gave him an extra-special doggy treat.

"Hooray for Pepper!" laughed Jimmy. "Your
barking really saved the day." That night, Pepper
was even allowed to sleep on Jimmy's bed.

And from that day on, Pepper decided that it was
best if he kept his bark for special occasions!

CUDDLES
to the Rescue

Cuddles was a very smart little poodle. Her hair was snowy white and fell in perfect curls. Her claws were always neatly trimmed and polished. She wore a crisp red bow on top of her head. And she never, ever went out without her sparkly dog collar.

Once a week Cuddles was sent to the Poodle Parlour, where she was given a wash, cut and blow dry. And every morning her owner, Gilly, brushed and styled Cuddles' hair until they both looked exactly the same!

But although Cuddles was the smartest, most pampered pooch around, she was not happy. You see, she didn't have any doggy friends.

Whenever Gilly took her walking in the park, Cuddles tried her best to make friends but the other dogs didn't want to know her.

"Here comes Miss Snooty," they would bark.
Then they'd point and snigger, before racing away to
have some playful puppy fun.

And Cuddles was never
let off her velvet lead. "Those
other dogs look rough,"
explained Gilly. "You're far
safer walking with me."

Cuddles would have loved to
run around with the other dogs. She thought that
chasing sticks and balls looked like brilliant fun. And
she was sure that she'd be able to swim in the lake if
only Gilly would let her.

But the other dogs didn't
know that Cuddles wanted
to be one of them. They
just took one look at her
snowy white curls and
sparkly collar and thought
that she was too posh for them.

"She doesn't want to get her paws dirty," Mrs
Collie explained to Skip, her youngest pup, when he
asked why Cuddles was always
on a lead.

Then one day, Cuddles
was walking with Gilly in
the park, when she saw
Skip chasing ducks beside
the lake.

Cuddles looked around but Mrs Collie was
nowhere to be seen.

"Be careful!" barked Cuddles, as Skip bounced up
and down with excitement

But Skip was far too busy to listen. Then, as a
duck took off, Skip took an extra large bounce, and
threw himself into the lake.

"Stop!" barked Cuddles. But it was no good,
Skip was already up to his chin in water.

"Help! Help!" barked Skip, as he splashed about
wildly in the lake.

Cuddles looked around, but no one else had noticed the little pup in the water. She gave a loud bark, and then, using all her strength, pulled the lead from Gilly's hand.

"Cuddles!" cried Gilly. But Cuddles was already in the water. Gilly looked on in horror as Cuddles caught the struggling pup by the scruff of his neck and dragged him ashore.

Once on dry land, Cuddles gave herself a big shake, then started to lick Skip dry.

"Cuddles," breathed Skip, who was quickly recovering from his ordeal.

"Cuddles!" cried Gilly, pointing in horror at her soaking wet curls and muddy paws.

"Will you play with me?" barked Skip, wagging his tail hopefully.

Cuddles looked at Gilly, then at Skip. Surely Gilly wouldn't mind just this once.

Gilly looked in amazement as Cuddles raced Skip across the park to find Mrs Collie. She had never seen Cuddles look so scruffy. But, much more importantly, she had never seen her look so happy.

After that, Gilly always let Cuddles play with the other dogs in the park. But she always made sure that she had an extra big wash and brush when she got home. But Cuddles didn't mind. She had so many doggy friends that she was the happiest little poodle around.

— Ebby the —
SMALLEST
— Pup —

Ebby was the smallest puppy in the litter. His brothers and sisters were all bigger than he was. He wouldn't have minded, but they were always teasing him.

"Out the way, titch!" they laughed, as they pushed him to the side at meal times.

"Last one's a baby," they barked, as they rushed out to play. And, of course, Ebby lost every time.

"You're small because you were the last to be born," explained his mum. "And that's why you're so special." But Ebby didn't feel very special. In fact, he just felt sad.

One day, a family came to see the puppies. "Look smart," said their mother. "They've come to take one of you home."

Of course, all the puppies wanted to be chosen but only one could go – and it wasn't Ebby.

After that, lots of people came to the house. Each of them left with a puppy of their own, but nobody chose Ebby. Eventually, Ebby was the only puppy left.

"Nobody wants me," sniffed Ebby. "I'm not as good as other dogs."

"Don't be silly," said his mum. "You're just special, you'll see."

The next day, a little girl came to the house. "Oh, goody! They saved him for me," she laughed.

Ebby looked around to see who she was talking about. But, of course, nobody else was there.

Suddenly, Ebby was lifted into the air and whirled around. "You are the cutest puppy in the whole wide world!" smiled the little girl.

Ebby felt a bit giddy but he smiled back anyway. It seemed that somebody did want him, after all.

"I wonder where we're going," thought Ebby, as he waved goodbye to his mum. But he soon found out because his new home was just next door!

Ebby quickly settled into his new home. Helen, his new owner, loved him with all her heart, and Ebby loved her too. She gave him his favourite food and she played with him all the time. And, best of all, Ebby could still see his mum through the garden gate.

When Ebby was old enough, Helen and her daddy took him for a walk in the woods. Ebby hadn't been out before so he was very pleased when his mum came too. There were other dogs walking in the woods and Ebby felt shy. He hid behind his mum. He didn't want everyone to see how small he was.

Suddenly, something small and soft hurtled into him. "Hiya, titch!" barked a familiar voice. It was his biggest brother, but he seemed to have shrunk. He was only as high as Ebby's shoulder.

"He hasn't shrunk," laughed his mum, when

Ebby whispered in her ear. "You've grown, silly. It's all that food Helen gives you."

After that, Ebby and his brother had great fun playing together. They had even more fun when they were joined by two of their sisters.

Their mum watched proudly as they raced around the trees. And she couldn't help smiling when Ebby turned around and barked, "Last one's a baby!"

The NAUGHTY — Kitten —

Ginger was a naughty little kitten. He didn't always mean to be naughty, but somehow things just turned out that way.

"You really should be more careful," warned Mummy. But Ginger was too busy getting into trouble to listen.

One day, Ginger was in a particularly playful mood. First, he tried to play tag with his smallest sister – and chased her right up an old apple tree. It took Daddy all morning to get her down.

Then, Ginger dropped cream all over the dog's tail. The dog whirled round and round as he tried to lick it off. He got so dizzy that he fell right over. That really made Ginger laugh until his sides hurt.

After that, Ginger thought it would be fun to play hide-and-seek with the mice. He frightened them so much that they refused to come out of their hole for the rest of the day.

Then, Ginger crept up behind the rabbit and shouted, "HI!" The poor rabbit was so surprised that he fell head-first into his breakfast. Ginger thought he looked ever so funny covered in lettuce leaves. The rabbit was very cross.

For his next trick, Ginger knocked over a

wheelbarrow full of apples while he was trying to fly like a bird. He really couldn't help laughing when the apples knocked his little brother flying into the air.

And when one of the

apples splashed into the garden pond, Ginger decided
to go apple bobbing. How he laughed as the goldfish
bumped into each other in their hurry to get out of
his way.

Ginger laughed so much that, WHO-OO-AH! he
began to lose his balance. He stopped laughing as he
tried to stop himself falling into the pond. But,
SPLASH! it was no good – he fell right in.

"Help! I can't swim," wailed Ginger, splashing wildly around. But he needn't have worried, the water only reached up to his knees. "Yuck!" he moaned, squirting out a mouthful of water.

"Ha, ha, ha!" laughed the other kittens, who had come to see what the noise was about. And the dog and the rabbit soon joined in.

"You really should be more careful," said Mummy, trying not to smile.

"It's not funny," said Ginger. He gave the other animals a hard glare as Daddy pulled him out of the pond. But then he caught sight of his reflection in the water. He did look very funny. Soon he was laughing as loud as the others.

After that, Ginger tried hard not to be quite so naughty. And do you know what? He even succeeded ...some of the time!

— Where's —
WANDA?

Sally was worried. Wanda, her cat, was getting fat. She was behaving very strangely, too. She wouldn't go in her basket.

"She must be ill," Sally told her mummy. "Her tummy's all swollen, and she hasn't slept in her basket for days."

"Don't worry," said Mummy, giving Sally a hug. "If she's not better in the morning, we'll take her to the vet."

"Sssh!" whispered Sally. "You know how much Wanda hates the V-E-T." But it was too late, Wanda had already gone.

Sally and her mummy searched high and low but they couldn't find Wanda anywhere. She didn't even come running when they left out a saucer of milk.

Wanda was still missing the following morning.

"She must have heard us talking about the vet," said Sally, as they searched around the house.

They found all sorts of things they thought they had lost in the house, including Teddy, who was hiding under the sofa. But Wanda was nowhere to be seen.

"Perhaps she's hiding in the garden," said Sally.

They looked in the flowerbed, under the hedge, and up the tree. But all they found there were the birds.

"Sometimes she sunbathes in the vegetable patch," said Sally. But the only animal there was a fluffy rabbit.

"Wanda!" called Mummy, looking in the shed. Wanda often liked sleeping in there. But today all they found there were the mice.

"Maybe she's been locked in the garage," said Sally. So they found the keys and searched inside. They looked around the car. They looked in the car.

They even looked under the car. But all they found there were the spiders.

Wanda was nowhere around the house or garden, so Mummy took Sally to look in the park.

"Here, Wanda!" called Sally. But all they found there were dogs. Wanda hated dogs, so she wouldn't be there.

On the way home, they peeped over hedges and peered behind dustbins. Sally even sat on Mummy's shoulders so that she could look on top of people's garages and sheds. But Wanda was nowhere to be seen. She had disappeared.

"She must have run away," cried Sally. "We're never going to find her."

But Mummy had an idea. She helped Sally to draw some pictures of Wanda. Then they wrote MISSING and their telephone number on the pictures. They posted the leaflets through all the letterboxes in the street.

Later that afternoon, Sally and her mummy were sitting in the garden when Mrs Jones from next door popped her head over the hedge.

"Come and see what I've found in my laundry basket," smiled Mrs Jones.

Sally and her mummy rushed next door at once. When Sally saw what Mrs Jones had in her laundry basket she couldn't believe her eyes.

There, sitting amongst the washing, was Wanda. She looked very slim and very proud. And beside her lay five tiny kittens. They were so young that their eyes were still closed. Wanda hadn't been ill after all. She'd been expecting kittens!

Mrs Jones said that they could keep the basket until Wanda had finished with it. So Mummy carried the new family home as Sally skipped beside her.

Sally was so excited. She just couldn't wait to tell people how they'd gone searching for one cat and found six!

— Fierce —
TIGER

Tiger wasn't really a tiger. He was a fierce stray kitten. People called him Tiger because he hissed and arched his back whenever they came near.

"You really should be nicer to people," said his friend Tibbles. "They're not so bad once you train them."

But Tiger didn't trust people. If they came too near, he would show his claws and even give them a scratch. That soon taught them not to mess with Tiger.

Tiger looked after himself. He didn't need anyone. At night he wandered the streets, searching dustbins for scraps and stealing food put out for pets. And during the day, he slept wherever he could – sometimes under a bush, sometimes on top of a garage, and sometimes under the cars in an old scrap yard.

One cold winter's night, Tiger was wandering the streets when it began to snow. He spotted an open window.

"Aha," thought Tiger. "I bet it's warm and dry in there." He jumped through the window and found himself in a dark porch.

"This will do," thought Tiger. So he curled into a ball

and was soon fast asleep. He was so comfortable that he slept all through the night.

When he finally woke up, there was no one around. But beside him was a bowl of food and a dish of water.

"Don't mind if I do," purred Tiger. He gobbled down the whole lot, then drank some water before leaving through the window again.

That day was colder than any Tiger had ever known, so when night fell and he saw the window open once more, he didn't hesitate to sneak in. This time, Tiger could see that the door from the porch was slightly ajar. He pushed it open and found himself in a warm kitchen. So he settled down and had a wonderful night's sleep.

When he awoke in the morning, he found a bowl of delicious fish and a dish of water beside him.

"Don't mind if I do," purred Tiger. And he wolfed down the fish and lapped up the water before leaving.

That night it was still snowing. Tiger returned once more. This time, when he went to settle himself beside the fire, he found a cosy basket there.

"Don't mind if I do," purred Tiger. And he crawled in and went to sleep. Tiger had never slept so well.

In the morning, Tiger was woken by a rattling sound. Someone was in the kitchen.

Tiger opened his left eye just a crack. A little boy was placing a bowl beside the basket.

Tiger opened his eyes and stared at the little boy. The little boy stared at Tiger. Tiger leapt to his feet and got ready to hiss and scratch.

"Good boy," whispered the little boy, gently.

Tiger looked at the bowl. It was full of milk. "Don't mind if I do," he purred, and he drank the lot.

After that, Tiger returned to the house every night. Before long, he never slept anywhere else. The little boy always gave him plenty to eat and drink. And in return, Tiger let the little boy stroke him and hold him on his lap.

One morning, Tiger was playing with the little boy in the garden, when his old friend Tibbles strolled past.

"Hello Tiger," meowed Tibbles. "I thought you didn't like people!"

"Oh," smiled Tiger, "they're okay once you've trained them."

Tiger was no longer a fierce stray kitten!

— A Home —
FOR ARCHIE

Archie, the black and white kitten, wasn't pleased. His owner, Tessa, hadn't given him his favourite fish for breakfast. All he had in his dish when he looked was some biscuits left over from the day before.

"Out you go," said Tessa, who was busy mopping the kitchen floor. And she pushed Archie out the door.

Now Archie was quite cross. He flicked his tail and swished his head. "I know when I'm not wanted," he thought. "I'll find someone who knows how to look after me!"

He jumped onto the garden fence and dropped into the neighbour's garden. Mrs Green always gave him a treat.

But as soon as his paws touched the ground, he heard a loud bark. Archie had forgotten about Bouncer, Mrs Green's playful new puppy.

Bouncer raced across the lawn and started to bounce around Archie.

"It's far too rough here," thought Archie, scrambling up a handy tree.

He jumped into the next garden. It belonged to Mr Reed. He didn't have a playful dog.

Archie strolled across the lawn and jumped up onto a window ledge. He was just about to squeeze through the open window, when he heard a squawk, followed by, "Who's a pretty boy?" Archie had forgotten about Mr Reed's parrot.

"It's far too noisy here," thought Archie. He made a quick escape through the hedge.

The next garden belonged to Granny Smith. She lived on her own and didn't have any pets.

"Meow!" called Archie. Granny Smith always had something nice to eat.

"Pussy!" cried a little voice from inside. Archie stopped in his tracks as he heard the patter of little feet running along the hall carpet. Oh, dear! Granny Smith's grandson was visiting. He always pulled Archie's tail. Archie decided to disappear before he got outside.

Archie squeezed through a broken panel in the fence. The next garden was rather overgrown. Some new people had just moved in and Archie hadn't met them yet. He hoped they liked kittens.

Archie strolled towards the house. He hadn't got far before he heard a hiss behind him. He turned around just in time to see a Siamese cat preparing to pounce. Archie, who knew better than to get in a fight with a Siamese, didn't stop to say hello. He flew through the grass, leapt onto the fence and ran as fast as his paws would carry him.

"I don't think I'll bother going there again," thought Archie, when he stopped for breath. He sat on the fence and thought what to do next. As he sat there, a wonderful fish smell drifted past. Archie sniffed and followed his nose, his tail twitching at the thought of a wonderful fish breakfast.

Archie wandered past garden after garden where children screamed, birds squawked, dogs barked and cats wailed. At last his nose gave an extra big twitch. He stopped by a garden that was wonderfully quiet.

"Archie, there you are!" a voice called. It was Tessa. "I've finished cleaning, and I've got a lovely piece of fish for you!"

Archie purred. "Good old Tessa!" he thought. "She does know how to look after me, after all!"

— Shanty —
GOES TO SEA

Shanty, the harbour kitten, just loved fish. He ate
every scrap that the fishermen threw away.
And sometimes, when nobody was looking, he even
helped himself to a few whole fish that should have
gone to market.

"Don't you ever get tired of fish?" asked his friend Gull. But Shanty just shook his head and continued nibbling on a tasty sardine. He just couldn't get enough fish!

One day, Shanty had a brilliant idea. "There's only one thing that would be better than being a harbour kitten," he told Gull. "And that would be being a boat kitten. Then I could eat all the fish I wanted."

So the next morning, when none of the fishermen were looking, Shanty crept aboard the *Salty Sardine*, the biggest of all the fishing boats in the harbour. The sailors were so busy that they didn't notice the stowaway hidden beneath an old raincoat.

The sea was calm as the boat chugged out to sea, and Shanty had a great time dreaming about all the fish he was going to eat.

When the fishermen started pulling in the nets, Shanty couldn't believe his eyes. He was in kitten heaven. He'd never seen so many fish. There were mackerel. There were cod. There were haddock. And there were Shanty's favourite, sardines.

There were so many that nobody noticed when a few began to disappear under the old raincoat. And they didn't notice when the bones were thrown out the other side.

Shanty ate and ate, until he could eat no more. Then he curled up and settled down to sleep. But just as he was dozing off, something strange began to happen.

The *Salty Sardine* began to creak and moan. Then it began to sway and rock. Water sprayed over the sides as it bounced over the waves then crashed back down again. The *Salty Sardine* rode up and down the rough sea.

Shanty's head began to reel and his stomach began to roll. Oh, how he wished he hadn't eaten so many fish! Oh, how he wished he had stayed on dry land!

"We're going to drown," wailed Shanty, as a big wave crashed over him and the raincoat.

Soaked right through, Shanty peered out to see what the fishermen were doing. He couldn't believe his eyes. Instead of running about and screaming, they were carrying on with their work. One of them, who Shanty thought must be the captain, was even whistling. And another was eating a sausage roll. It seemed that for them, this was a normal day's work.

When the *Salty Sardine* finally got back to the harbour, Shanty couldn't get off fast enough.

"How is life as a boat kitten?" asked Gull, when he came visiting later that evening.

"Ah!" said Shanty, after he'd finished nibbling on a scrap of sardine. "Boats are all very well but give me the harbour any day. After all, how many fish can one kitten eat!"

Sleepy the FARM KITTEN

Sleepy, the farm kitten, was always tired. He liked nothing better than sleeping all day long, and all through the night. While all the other kittens were busy chasing mice or scaring away birds, he was normally fast asleep.

"Looks too much like hard work to me," he'd yawn, before strolling off to find a comfy spot for a snooze.

One day, while the other kittens were chasing mice around the corn shed, Sleepy stretched and looked around for somewhere to nap.

"You can't sleep here," said the farmer's wife, sweeping Sleepy out of the kitchen with a broom. "Today's cleaning day and you'll just be in the way."

"You can't sleep here," clucked the hens, flapping him out of the chicken run. "We're laying eggs and we certainly don't want you watching."

"You can't sleep here," mooed the cows, shooing him out of the milking shed. "We're busy being milked, and a kitten can never be trusted around milk."

"You can't sleep here," said the farmer, pushing him out of the dairy. "We're making ice-cream and we don't want your hairs all over the place."

"I'm really tired," Sleepy complained to a passing mouse. "Can I sleep with you mice?"

"Don't be ridiculous," laughed the mouse. "Don't you know that kittens are supposed to chase mice?"

Just as Sleepy was about to give up hope of ever finding somewhere to sleep, he spotted the ideal bed. There was a soft bale of hay sitting on a trailer.

"Purrfect," he purred, curling into a sleepy ball. Within seconds, he was purring away in his sleep.

He was so comfortable, that he didn't even wake up when the tractor pulling the trailer chugged into life. And he still didn't wake up when the tractor and trailer bumped down the road leading to town.

155

It was only when the trailer shuddered to a halt that Sleepy woke with a start. He blinked his eyes sleepily, stretched, and looked around. Then he flew to his feet. He couldn't believe his eyes. He was at the market and the farmer was driving the trailer away with the tractor.

"Wait for me," meowed Sleepy, leaping down from the trailer. But the farmer had gone. "Looks like I'll have to walk all the way home," moaned

Sleepy, as he started to walk back towards the farm.

Sleepy walked all afternoon and all through the night. The cockerel was just beginning to crow the morning in when Sleepy finally made it back in through the farmyard gate.

"Hello, lazybones," called the other kittens when they saw him. "Where have you been sleeping all night while we've been chasing mice?"

But for once Sleepy really was tired. He was far too tired to explain where he had been all night. And it wasn't long before he was fast asleep!

Sparky and the
BABY DRAGON

Sparky was a young dragon who lived in a cave far, far away. Now, as you know, dragons can breathe flames out of their noses! But you may not know that baby dragons have to *learn* how to do it.

"Watch me," said Mum to Sparky, and she puffed out a long flame and lit a candle.

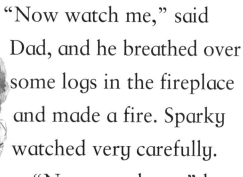

"Now watch me," said Dad, and he breathed over some logs in the fireplace and made a fire. Sparky watched very carefully.

"Now watch *me*," he said, and he puffed until he was purple in the face. Two or three little sparks came out of his nose and ears!

"Bravo!" said Dad.

"It's coming on!" said Mum.

Sparky felt very proud.

One day Mum and Dad had to go out.

"Stay indoors," they told Sparky. "*Don't* go out, and *don't* let anybody in!"

"Why?" asked Sparky.

"Because of the wicked witch," said Mum. "She hates little dragons and turns them into teapots, just for fun!"

"Oh!" said Sparky. But he didn't mind staying in. He had some new toy knight figures to play with.

He had just started when he heard a bell outside.

"Ting-a-ling," it went, "ting-a-ling." And then a voice said, "Ice cream! Ice cream! Come and get your ice cream!"

Sparky peeped out. Outside was a brightly painted ice cream cart. Sitting behind the wheel was an old woman with a big grin.

"Come and get your ice cream, Sparky," said the woman, and she laughed!

It was a loud, cackling laugh. When Sparky heard it, he knew it was the witch. He slammed the door and locked it.

The witch pedalled off in a rage.

"Phew!" thought Sparky, as he settled down to his knights and dragons game. "That was close."

The afternoon passed peacefully.

Then, the doorbell rang. "Who is it?" Sparky called out.

"It's Uncle Jack," said a voice, "I've come to take you fishing."

Sparky liked Uncle Jack, and he liked fishing! He went to open the door. Then he stopped.

"Is it really you?" he asked.

"Of course it is," laughed Uncle Jack.

But, as soon as Sparky heard the loud, cackling

laugh, he knew it was the witch.

"Go away!" he shouted.

"Go away!"

Then he heard someone crying. He peered through the door and saw a baby dragon on the doorstep!

"I've lost my mummy!" sobbed the dragon.

"You'd better come in," said Sparky. He opened the door! The baby dragon rushed in! Then …

"Got you!" snapped the baby dragon. And turned into the witch!

Sparky gasped.

The witch raised her wand and shouted the magic word 'Ta-ra-ra-boom-de-ay!' and started to spin very fast.

Sparky closed his eyes and puffed as hard as he could. When he opened them he had a big surprise! The witch was surrounded by a puff of smoke.

Sparky watched in amazement as smoke cleared. Then, would you believe it, *she had turned herself into a bright, blue teapot!*

Just then Mum and Dad came back.

"Have you had any trouble while we've been away?" asked Mum, kissing him.

"Not much!" said Sparky. "But, next time you go out, can I come with you?"

"Of course you can!" said Mum. "Now why don't I make some tea in this nice new teapot!"

BoINK

Boink was a small round monster. His name was Boink, but it was also the sound he made when he moved around. You and I can walk and run, but Boink the monster bounced like a ball – BOINK! BOINK! BOINK! – until he got where he was going.

He looked like a space-hopper toy and he was rubbery too, to help him bounce.

Boink lived happily in an empty dog kennel at the bottom of Joe's garden. No one knew he was there. He couldn't even remember how he had got there, but that didn't worry him. Boink didn't worry about anything. He was a happy little monster and he enjoyed life. There was just one problem – he didn't have anything to play with.

Boink often watched Joe playing. Joe didn't have anyone to play with but he had lots of toys. Boink watched him as he took all his cars out of a big green box. He watched as he lined up all the red cars together, then all the blue cars, and then all the yellow cars. He watched as he moved the cars around. When Joe did this he made a strange sound.

"Brmmm! Brmmm!" he went, "Brmmm! Brmmm! Brmmm!"

Boink practised making the noise at night when no one was listening.

"Brmmm!" he said softly, and then louder, "Brmmm! Brmmm!" But it wasn't any fun without the cars. Boink wanted some toys of his own. So he decided to borrow some!

One night, when Joe was asleep, Boink bounced in through an open window. In Joe's bedroom there were toys everywhere. There were aeroplanes on a shelf and a train set on the floor. Boink took two cars out of the green box. Then he bounced out of the window and back to the dog kennel.

The first thing Joe noticed the next morning was that some of his cars were missing.

"Mum," he called, "have you seen my cars?"

But Joe's mum hadn't seen them. The next day Joe whizzed around the garden with his aeroplanes going, "Neeaw! Neeaw!"

Boink watched Joe playing, and that night he took two aeroplanes from Joe's bedroom!

"Mum," said Joe, going into the kitchen, "my aeroplanes are missing!"

"Did you leave them in the garden?" asked Mum. But Joe knew he hadn't. Joe had to play with his train set instead.

That night Joe only pretended to go to sleep. He couldn't believe his eyes! He saw a roly-poly monster bounce in through the window and take his train set! As Boink bounced back out of the window Joe leapt out of bed and watched him disappear with the train set into the old kennel.

The next day, after breakfast, Joe went straight to the dog kennel and peeped inside. There, fast asleep, was a roly-poly monster. And all around him were Joe's missing toys! Joe was so surprised, he gave a startled yelp. Boink woke up.

"Brmmm! Brmmm!" said Boink grinning.

"What do you mean, Brmmm! Brmmm!?" said Joe.

"Neeaw! Neeaw!" said Boink.

"You only say Brmmm! Brmmm! when you're playing with cars," said Joe. "And you only say Neeaw! Neeaw! when you're playing aeroplanes."

"Neeaw! Neeaw!" said Boink.

"You can play with me if you like," said Joe, "but you must promise never to take my toys without asking."

"Chuff! Chuff!" said Boink.

"Right then, let's join up all the railway lines so that we can play with the train set," said Joe.

"Toot! Toot!" said Boink.

And that's what they did. When they had finished, the train set went in and out of the kennel and the engine went round and round.

When Joe's mum looked out of the window, she was pleased to see that Joe had found his missing toys. And she was surprised to see a space-hopper in the garden!

NESSY
of the Lake

Nessy was a very shy monster. She was also very big. She was so big she could fill a swimming pool! Luckily, she lived in a large, deep lake, so no one ever saw her.

Nessy was too shy to go out and make friends. She once tried making friends with a small fish, but the fish bit her nose and swam away! Nessy shrugged. She was fed up. She hoped she'd find a friend soon.

One lovely sunny day Nessy peeped above the surface and saw a small boy fishing with his grandpa on the bank. The boy had a rod and a net and a shiny, red bucket.

He fished all day but didn't catch anything.

The next day Nessy watched again.

The little boy still didn't catch any fish.

"Watch out for ripples on the surface of the lake, Billy," said his grandpa. "Ripples mean fish!" Then Billy's grandpa nodded off to sleep.

Billy watched the surface of the lake for signs of ripples. Nessy watched Billy. All was quiet and still.

Then Nessy decided to go a bit closer … and closer … and closer still.

Billy stared at the ripples on the lake. He watched them coming closer … and closer … and closer still.

"Boo!" said Nessy suddenly splashing her head out of the water.

"Wow!" said Billy, staring. "You're not a fish – you're a monster!"

Nessy tried a friendly smile, showing all her teeth.

"Are you going to eat me?" asked Billy, alarmed.

"Of course not," said Nessy. "I want to be friends."

"You've got lots of big teeth," said Billy.

"Have I?" said Nessy. "Do they frighten you?"

"Not when you smile," said Billy.

Nessy smiled even wider.

"My name's Billy," said Billy. "What's yours?"

"Nessy," said Nessy. "What are you doing?" she asked Billy.

"I'm trying to catch a fish, but I'm not having much luck."

"I'll help," said Nessy. "Leave it to me!" and she started swimming very fast into the middle of the lake.

Then she disappeared! Billy stared at the middle of the lake. He stared for ages. Then the next thing he heard was Grandpa's voice saying, "Wake up, Billy!"

"I am awake," said Billy. "You'll never guess who I've been talking to, Grandpa!"

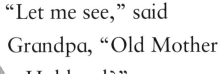

"Let me see," said Grandpa, "Old Mother Hubbard?"

"No," said Billy, "of course not."

"The Three Bears?"

"Grandpa!"

"Who then?"

"Nessy, of course, the monster who lives in the lake!"

"You've been dreaming, Billy!" smiled Grandpa.

"No I haven't," said Billy. "She came really close. And she splashed me, although she didn't mean to. Look … my shoes are all wet!" Grandpa looked.

"And she said she'd help me catch a fish," Billy went on.

"Well, it's time to go now,

Billy!" said Grandpa. "Don't forget your bucket!"

Billy picked up his bucket.

"Grandpa!" he said. "Look!"

Grandpa looked. There in Billy's bucket was the prettiest blue and gold fish he had ever seen.

"Well, I'll be blowed," said Grandpa.

Billy just grinned. Gently, he tipped the fish back into the water. Then he called out loudly, "See you, Nessy! See you tomorrow!"

And from the middle of the lake a big, shy monster waved back.

SNIFFLE

A long way away, in a jungle no one had ever been to before, lived the Sniffle monster. The famous explorer, Major Jolly, went into the jungle looking for new animals. First, he found a big, bright bird that strutted about showing everyone what a great tail it had. Then he found a new type of monkey that could knit socks! His greatest discovery, though, was when he came upon the MONSTER, in a tree, eating a banana.

Major Jolly got very excited! The monster was intelligent! That means it could think like you and me. Major Jolly knew it was intelligent because only intelligent people eat bananas. Don't you think so? Well Major Jolly did, because he liked bananas too.

The monster was quite ugly, but then he would be, wouldn't he. He was big, ugly and covered in red fur. His fingertips could touch the floor when he was standing on the table!

Major Jolly decided to take him home to show his wife. They flew back in a big plane and the monster sat on three seats as well as a passenger. The famous explorer's wife met them at the airport.

"This is the monster I discovered, Maud," said Major Jolly. "He doesn't speak English."

"How do you do?" Maud held out her hand.

"Howdeedoodee," repeated the monster. He took the lady's hand and sniffed it, and then danced her round the room in circles.

"I'll soon have him speaking English," said Maud, as they danced past for the third time.

Back home the monster wanted to dance with everyone at first! But just a few weeks later he began to look ill and sad. He coughed and sniffed and spluttered. His coat turned dull, and patches of fur fell out. And he had something really nasty running out of his nose. He spent all day trying to lie on the sofa without falling off.

When Maud visited, he wouldn't dance round the room with her. "My dear Monster," she said, "what's wrong with you?"

The monster had learned to speak by now.

"I am Sniffle monster!" he said. "I was taken away from jungle without friend. I must have this friend with me always, or I get ill! Stuff comes out of my nose! My friend is Hanky monster.

Maud thought she understood.

"And you need this Hanky monster … umm… to wipe your nose for you?"

"No, no, no!" said Sniffle. "Hanky is a magician. He will make Sniffle dance again! Only Hanky monster knows secret magic potion."

Major Jolly was really sorry that he had taken the Sniffle monster away from his Hanky monster. They must go back to the jungle straight away, find the Hanky monster, and Sniffle would be well again. Just a few days later, they found the place in the jungle where Major Jolly had camped before. Suddenly, something that looked like a giant cabbage hurtled through the bushes and threw itself at Sniffle. Sniffle gave a whoop of joy! The cabbage and Sniffle danced round the clearing until Sniffle was too tired to move. The cabbage was the Hanky monster, of course! It rushed back into the jungle.

"Gone to get magic potion," whispered Sniffle weakly.

The Hanky monster came back with a drink in a coconut shell. Sniffle drank it and went straight to bed. Next morning his coat was shiny and his nose had stopped running. He danced with everyone.

The secret potion was amazing! Sniffle was well again. Major Jolly was desperate to know the secret of the magic drink.

"It's a secret!" was all the Hanky monster would say. But when Major Jolly got home there was a letter for him with SECRET MAGIC POTION – DON'T TELL ANY PEOPLE! written on the outside. He opened the letter eagerly. A photograph of Sniffle and Hanky fell out. The letter read ...

HOT LEMON AND HONEY!

– The Fluff –
MONSTERS

This is the story of the Fluff monsters. Everyone has seen fluff under the bed. That's because the Fluff monsters live under beds. They need beds that are not too clean underneath.

The Fluff monsters only come out when it's dark. They don't know what the world outside beds is like in daylight. They think it's scary just being out during the day. Who knows what might be out in the daylight? Once, Fluff-boy was having a quiet

meal eating fluff and custard, when suddenly *the-magic-sucking-thing* appeared. It made a terrible noise as it came closer and closer. Then a tube with a brush on the end sucked up all the fluff under the bed after he'd spent ages collecting it!

But Fluff-boy had only ever lived under his bed. He wanted to know what it was like under other beds.

"Only naughty Fluff monsters go out in daylight," said Fluff-mummy, "and do you know what happens to naughty Fluff monsters?"

"No, I don't," said Fluff-boy, alarmed. "What?"

His mother put on a scary voice and said, *"The Little Girl will get you!"*

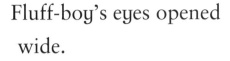

Fluff-boy's eyes opened wide.

"Who's the Little Girl?" he asked.

"The Little Girl is a monster who lives *in the bed!*" said Fluff-mummy. "She is really clean and pretty! She will take you away and wash you and put you in a room with sun shining through the windows! She will open the doors and fill the room with fresh air from *outside!*"

"That's horrible! I don't believe you," said Fluff-boy. "You're making it up!"

"Well, you'll just have to be good," said Fluff-mummy, "or you'll find out!"

"Well, I'm not scared of the Little Girl!" said Fluff-boy.

Fluff-boy wasn't going to be put off. He wanted

to know what it was like under other beds. One day, while everyone was asleep, Fluff-boy slipped away. Outside, bright sunlight filled the room.

"That must be the window Fluff-mummy told me about," thought Fluff-boy.

He wandered into the next room and found another bed to slide under. There were spiders and daddy-long-legs, cobwebs and lots and lots of fluff! It was perfect! So Fluff-boy ate some fluff (though he did miss his mum's home-made custard) and settled into his new home.

But Fluff-boy couldn't sleep, as he was thinking about the Little Girl. He had to see if she was real or not. Plucking up courage he poked his head out from under the bed. Carefully, he climbed up the bed covers until he could scramble over the top.

Suddenly, the Little Girl woke and sat up. Fluff-boy was so surprised he jumped with fright.

"Aaargh!" shrieked Fluff-boy.

"Aaargh!" screamed the Little Girl.

They scrambled to each end of the bed and stared at each other.

"You gave me a fright!" said Fluff-boy.

"*Me* frighten *you*?" said the Little Girl. "*You* frightened *me!*"

"Did I?" said Fluff-boy. "Why?"

"Well, you're the Bogeyman aren't you?" said the Little Girl.

"There's no such thing as the Bogeyman,"

laughed Fluff-boy. "I'm Fluff-boy. I've just moved in under this bed. Do you live in this bed too?"

"No, silly," said the Little Girl. "I just sleep here at night. I thought scary Bogeymen lived under the bed. But you're not scary at all!"

"How about this then?" asked Fluff-boy. He stuck his thumbs in his ears, wiggled his fingers and poked his tongue out. The Little Girl laughed.

"That's not at all scary!" she said. "*This* is scary," and she pulled the corners of her mouth out with her fingers and crossed her eyes.

And that was how Fluff-boy and the Little Girl discovered that there is nothing scary under the bed or in it!

Wibble and the
EARTHLINGS

Wibble was from the planet Xog. He was on a mission. He'd been sent secretly to Earth to find out about Earthlings.

Wibble's spaceship wobbled on landing, but there wasn't too much damage. He radioed back to Xog to tell them his camera was broken.

"Just tell us what the Earthlings look like," said Captain Pimples, the leader of the Xogs, "and I'll draw them. Over!"

"I will," said Wibble. "Over and out!" He climbed down from the spaceship and looked around. There was a big sign saying ZOO.

"I wonder what that means," thought Wibble.

Wibble wobbled over to the nearest building and opened the door. He went up to a big wooden fence and saw his first Earthling. With its long neck, it leaned over the fence and gave Wibble a huge lick.

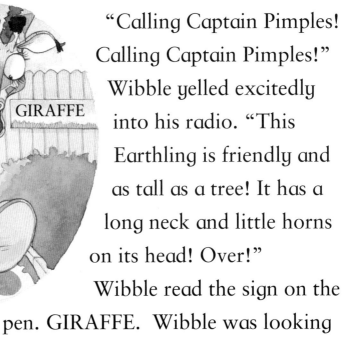

"Calling Captain Pimples! Calling Captain Pimples!" Wibble yelled excitedly into his radio. "This Earthling is friendly and as tall as a tree! It has a long neck and little horns on its head! Over!"

Wibble read the sign on the pen. GIRAFFE. Wibble was looking at a giraffe, of course, but because he didn't understand the signs, Wibble thought it must be an Earthling. Captain Pimples drew an Earthling with a long neck and two horns.

"Sounds okay so far!" said the captain. "Tell me more. Over!"

Wibble wandered to the next fence, marked ELEPHANT. He switched on the radio.

"It's an enormous Earthling! It has huge ears and a long spout on the front like a teapot! Over!"

Captain Pimples quickly added the big ears and the spout to his drawing.

Next, Wibble went into a building marked AQUARIUM. He gazed around at the water tanks.

One had a sign that said
SQUID. "This Earthling
has two huge eyes and
is covered in orange
spots! Over!" Wibble
said into his radio.
Captain Pimples
added two huge eyes
and orange spots to the
drawing.

"Okay!" said Captain Pimples. "We've heard
enough. Earthlings are big and hairy, have enormous

ears and a spout, two huge eyes, and orange spots.
A bit like us, really! Over and out!"

So Captain Pimples led an expedition to Earth.
That is when Mr Brown the zoo-keeper walked by.
Mr Brown got quite a shock when he saw them, but
not half as much as the Xogs did when they saw him.

"Aargh!" cried the Xogs, running back to their
spaceship. They took off and didn't stop until they
reached planet Xog. Captain Pimples found Earth on
his map, crossed it off and wrote underneath,
"BEWARE—MONSTERS!"

Susie and the
MERMAID

Today was Susie's birthday. Mum and Dad had given her a pretty sea-blue dress and shoes to match.

"Can I try them on now?" she asked.

"Of course, but don't get them dirty," warned her mum. Susie tried on the dress and shoes. They shimmered just like a mermaid's tail. Susie had always wanted to be a mermaid. She wandered down to Mermaid Rock and gazed out to sea, dreaming of what it would be like to be a mermaid.

"I'll make a birthday wish,"

194

thought Susie to herself. She closed her eyes. "I wish I could be a mermaid."

When she opened her eyes, she was no longer wearing her birthday dress – she had a mermaid's tail! Susie couldn't believe her luck! Her birthday wish had come true.

But then Susie heard someone crying. She looked around. There was someone sitting on the other side of Mermaid Rock wearing a blue dress just like Susie's new birthday dress!

"Why are you crying?" Susie asked the little girl.

"I'm crying because I've lost my tail," she replied. "You see, I'm a mermaid. But without my tail I can't go home!" As the mermaid cried, her tears splashed into the sea.

Susie suddenly realised what had happened. Her birthday wish must have made her swap places with the mermaid. Susie told the mermaid about her birthday wish.

"What can I do to change us back again?" asked Susie.

"If you can collect my tears from the sea, then you could wish again," said the mermaid.

Susie slipped into the sea. The water didn't feel a bit cold now that she was a mermaid. With her strong new tail she swam quickly to the bottom of the sea. But Susie didn't have any idea how to look for the mermaid's tears!

Susie asked the sea creatures to help her search for the tears. Crabs and fish, lobsters and winkles peered into holes and lifted up stones, but it was no use. They couldn't find a single tear. Susie didn't know what to do!

Then she heard, "One-two-three, one-two-three..." and from an underwater cave danced a large octopus wearing a long string of pearls! Its eight long arms whirled around as the octopus danced and twirled.

"Hello, little mermaid!" said the octopus.

"Can you help me?" asked Susie. "I'm looking for mermaid tears. But I don't know where to start."

"Ah! Well these pearls are just what you are looking for!" said the octopus. "That's what happens to mermaid tears you know – they turn into pearls! You can have them if you help me take them off!" laughed the octopus.

"Oh, thank you so much!" cried Susie untangling the pearls.

"Farewell, little mermaid!" laughed the octopus as it danced away, singing, "One-two-three, one-two-three ..."

Susie swam back to Mermaid Rock as quickly as

she could with the pearls. The mermaid was overjoyed. Susie closed her eyes and wished again. Instantly, she was wearing her blue dress and the mermaid had her tail back.

"Thank you, Susie," said the mermaid. "I hope I'll see you again."

Susie waved goodbye as the mermaid slipped into the sea and swam away. Susie hurried home for her birthday tea. She glanced down at her new blue dress to make sure it was still clean. Around the dress were sewn lots of tiny tear-shaped pearls!

Jade and the
JEWELS

Jade was the prettiest mermaid in the lagoon! Her hair was jet black and reached right down to the tip of her swishy, fishy tail. Her eyes were as green as emeralds, and her skin was as white as the whitest pearl. But Jade was so big-headed and vain that the other mermaids didn't like her!

"That Jade thinks too much of herself!" the other mermaids would say. "One of these days she'll come unstuck!"

There was one creature, though, who was fond of Jade, and that was Gentle, the giant turtle. He followed her wherever she went.

But Jade didn't even notice Gentle. She lived in a world of her own. She spent all her time combing her hair and admiring her reflection in the mirror.

One day Jade overheard the mermaids talking about a pirate ship that had sunk to the bottom of the ocean. On board was a treasure chest filled with precious jewels.

"But no one dares take the jewels," whispered the mermaids, "because the pirate ship is cursed!"

"I'm going to find that pirate ship," Jade told Gentle, "and the treasure chest!"

"But what about the curse?" asked Gentle.

"Oh, never mind that. Just imagine how beautiful I will look wearing all those jewels!" said Jade, and right away she set off.

"Wait for me!" called Gentle, paddling after her. "It's too dangerous to go alone!"

Jade swam to a deep part of the ocean she had never been to before. She dived through shoals of colourful fish, past the edge of the coral reef and deep, deep down to the very bottom of the ocean.

Finally, they found the shipwreck.

"Be careful, Jade," said Gentle. "Remember there is a curse on this pirate wreck."

"Nonsense," Jade told him. "I've come to get the jewels and I'm not going home without them!"

Jade searched the wreck until she saw the treasure chest through a porthole. Jade swam inside and reached out to touch the chest. The lid sprang open and brilliant jewels spilled over the sides. The colours were dazzling.

Jade lifted out a necklace and put it round her neck. There was a little gold and silver mirror in the chest. She held it up to admire her reflection. The necklace was beautiful! Jade looked lovelier than ever.

Suddenly, there was a loud crack, and the mirror shattered! Instantly the necklace turned to stone! It was the ship's curse!

Jade tried to take the necklace off, but she couldn't. She tried to swim, but the necklace was so heavy she couldn't move.

"Help!" Jade cried out. "Help! Help!" Gentle, the giant turtle, heard her and swam to the porthole.

"Help me, Gentle," she cried. "Please help me!"

"I warned you to be careful," said Gentle.

Jade began to cry. "I should have listened to you, Gentle," she sobbed.

Gentle's powerful flippers broke the necklace and freed Jade. As Jade and Gentle swam away from the wreck, Gentle said, "You don't need fancy jewels, Jade. You're pretty without them."

Once she was safely home, Jade told the other mermaids about the pirate ship curse.

"I've certainly learned my lesson," said Jade. "I'll never be vain again." And, from that day on, they were all friends. But Gentle was always her very best friend of all.

–The Naughty–
MERMAIDS

Of all the mermaids that lived in the sea, Jazz and Cassandra were the naughtiest. They were not supposed to swim above sea when there were people about. But their latest prank was to swim to the lighthouse and call out to the little boy who lived there.

"Coo-ee!" they would call and, when the little boy looked towards them, they giggled and dived under the waves.

"Coo-ee!" they called again from the other side of the lighthouse. Just as he ran round to see them, they dived under the waves again!

When King Neptune heard about it, he was very cross indeed!

"I won't have this naughty behaviour," he boomed. "Mermaids should not mix with children!"

But Jack, that was the boy's name, was lonely at the lighthouse. There was no one to play with. One day, Jack's mum made him a picnic. Jack laid the food on a cloth on the rocks. He had pizza and crisps and fizzy drink and chocolate.

The two naughty mermaids popped up from the waves. They soon spotted all the food.

"Hello!" they called to Jack. "Are you going to eat all this food by yourself?"

Jack was so surprised that he couldn't speak.
He'd never seen the mermaids before.

"Yes," said Jack, at last. "I mean, no! You can
have some of my picnic, if you like."

The mermaids had never had pizza or crisps or
fizzy drink or chocolate before. They ate so much
they felt quite sick! They swam home slowly, hoping
King Neptune wouldn't spot them. But he did! And
he summoned them to come and see him.

"Be warned!" said King Neptune. "Mermaids are
not like children. They cannot behave like children
and they cannot eat the food that children eat!"

For a while Jazz and Cassandra played with the other ocean creatures and ate mermaid food, like shrimps and seaweed. But they soon became bored!

"I'm longing for some pizza," said Jazz to Cassandra one day.

"So am I," answered Cassandra, "and some of those crispy things."

"Mmmm, and fizzy stuff!"

"And chocolate!"

The naughty mermaids looked at each other! Then, holding hands they swam up to the surface.

Jack was waiting for them with a picnic all ready. They ate and ate and ate. It all tasted so good. Afterwards they played hide-and -seek in the waves while Jack ran round the lighthouse trying to spot them. The mermaids enjoyed themselves so much, they came back the next day and the next.

On the third day, the mermaids said goodbye and started to swim to the bottom of the sea. But, oh dear! Their tails had become stiff and heavy. They could not move! King Neptune was right! Mermaids can't behave like children. They clung onto the rocks around the lighthouse and began to cry.

"What's wrong?" shouted Jack, alarmed.

"We're not supposed to eat children's food," they told him.

Jack knew exactly what to do! He got his net and bucket and searched the island, collecting shrimps and seaweed from the rock pools.

For three days and three nights he fed the mermaids proper mermaid food. By the end of the third day they could move their tails again and swim.

When they arrived home King Neptune was waiting for them. This time, King Neptune wasn't angry – he was glad to see them back safely.

"I hope you have learned a lesson," he said, quite gently. "Jack has been a good friend so you can play with him again. As long as you don't eat his food!"

From then on they saw quite a lot of their friend Jack, often going up to talk and play with him. But they never again ate Jack's food, except sometimes they had a piece of chocolate!

The Mermaid
IN THE POOL

John and Julia were on holiday at the seaside. Their mum and dad had found an amazing house with a big swimming pool. But, best of all, their bedroom overlooked the beach. It was perfect!

The first night there was a storm. The wind howled. The waves crashed over the beach and right up to the house. The children lay in bed listening to the storm outside.

By morning, the storm was over. The children woke early and looked out of their window. The garden furniture had blown over, there was seaweed all over the lawn and there was a mermaid in the swimming pool!

That's right! There was a mermaid in the swimming pool! The mermaid was swimming up and down the pool. John and Julia rushed outside but, when the mermaid saw them coming, she huddled in a corner of the pool. She was frightened.

"I'm sorry I swam into your blue pool," said the mermaid. "I didn't mean any harm!"

"It's okay!" said Julia gently. "We didn't mean to frighten you."

"That's right," said John. "We just wanted to meet you. We've never seen a mermaid before."

"My name is Marina," said the mermaid. "I was playing in the sea with my friend Blue, the dolphin, when the storm began. A huge wave washed me in, and now I'm stranded, and Blue is missing!"

"We'll help you look for Blue," said Julia at once. "We might be able to spot your friend from our bedroom window."

As soon as their mum and dad were safely out of the way, John and Julia found a wheelbarrow and wheeled Marina into the house.

"I've only had sky over my head before," said Marina. "The house won't fall on me will it?"

"Of course not," smiled John. They showed Marina all sorts of things she had never seen before. She thought the moving pictures on the television were weird. She thought Julia's teddy bear was wonderful, and that beds were the silliest things she had ever seen!

But, although they looked out of the window, there was no sign of Blue the dolphin in the sea.

"I have to go home soon!" Marina said sadly. "I can't stay out of the water for long, and I must find Blue. If only I hadn't lost my shell horn in the storm I could call him."

"We'll take you down to the sea," said John.

"And help you look for your shell," said Julia.

They lifted Marina back into the wheelbarrow and pushed her down to the beach. They spent the rest of the day searching for Marina's shell along the seashore. They had almost given up when, suddenly, Julia spotted a large shell half buried in the sand. John found a stick and dug it out. "It's my shell!"

cried Marina. They washed off the sand and Marina blew into it. The most beautiful sound drifted out across the waves. Straight away, there was an answering call! Far out to sea, they saw a streak of blue-grey. It was leaping high over the waves, swimming towards them. It was Blue, the dolphin!

Marina gave a cry of joy and swam to meet him. She flung her arms round his neck and hugged him. Then she turned to the watching children.

"Thank you for helping me," she called.

"See you next year!" called John and Julia. And they watched as Marina and Blue swam swiftly and smoothly together, back out to sea.

King Neptune's
DAY OFF

Trini the little mermaid worked in King
Neptune's palace. It was a beautiful palace,
with fountains and a statue of King Neptune in the
centre of the courtyard. Trini was happy working
there. But some fierce sharks guarded the palace.

Today it was King Neptune's birthday. King

Neptune called Trini to see him.

"I'm taking the day off," he said. "I'd like you to organise a birthday banquet for me this evening when I come back. So, until then, you will be in charge." And off he went!

The sharks were delighted! They thought they would have some fun while King Neptune was away.

"I'm in charge, so you must do as I say," Trini told them sternly, after the king had left.

The sharks just sniggered at her and didn't answer.

Trini set to work. She asked a team of fish to collect shrimps and special juicy seaweed. She told the crabs to collect smooth, pearly shells to use as plates. Then she sent her mermaid friends to collect pieces of coral to decorate the tables.

But the sharks were determined to make mischief and spoil everything. Before long they saw the fish carrying a net full of delicious food. "Give us that," they snapped, and in a few gulps the food was gone.

As soon as the crabs came back with their shell plates, the sharks took the shells and began throwing them to each other.

"Stop it at once!" cried Trini. But the sharks ignored her.

Then the sharks spotted the mermaids watching close by. They started to chase them all around the courtyard. "Stop it!" cried Trini. But the sharks just laughed and carried on chasing the mermaids.

Then Trini had an idea. She would trick the sharks! While they were chasing the mermaids, Trini squeezed through a crack in the hollow statue of King Neptune. The sharks were having great fun. The mermaids dropped all their pretty coral and swam away. The sharks couldn't stop laughing.

They gathered around King Neptune's statue to plan some more mischief.

Suddenly, a voice like thunder boomed, "Behold, it is I, King Neptune, Emperor of all the Seas and Oceans." The sharks were very frightened. Then the voice bellowed, "Do as Trini commands or you will be banished from the kingdom!"

Then the voice from inside the statue told the sharks to pick up the plates and fetch more food and lay the tables for the banquet. And, while they were busy, Trini crept out from inside the hollow statue where she had been hiding!

So Trini's banquet was a great success. Everyone was there, even the sharks! But they had to stand guard outside the palace, while everyone inside enjoyed the food, music and dancing. King Neptune had a marvellous time and asked Trini if she would always be his special helper.

"I'd be delighted," she answered, blushing!

- The -
MERMAID
- Fair -

Jason loved diving and he was very good at it. He loved to dive for shellfish and sponges, but mainly he loved to look for pearls. Pearls are jewels of the sea and he collected even the tiniest one.

One day Jason was diving when he saw a sign on a rock. Jason was very surprised. He swam closer and was even more surprised to read the words: MERMAID FAIR TODAY!

Jason had heard of mermaids, of course. But he'd never seen one! Jason took a huge gulp of air and swam towards the fair. He hid behind a rock and watched. Jason could hardly believe his eyes; there was a crowd of mermaids having fun at the fair. Some were riding dolphins, some were swimming in races and some were playing games at the stalls.

And there were pearls! There was a stall where you could win a pearl by throwing a hoop over it.

Another, where if you pulled a lever down and saw three shells in a row, a hundred white pearls came out of a hole at the bottom! Two of the mermaids noticed Jason watching and came over to him.

"You're a strange sort of fish!" teased the fair-haired mermaid.

"I think it must be a boy!" laughed the dark-haired mermaid.

"Hello," said Jason. To Jason's amazement, he found he could talk and breathe under water! "Can I take part in your fair? I'd love to win some pearls!"

"Oh, you don't want dull old pearls," said one.

"What you really want are these," and she opened her hand to show Jason a plastic comb! It was a pink plastic comb with a flower on it. The mermaid had found it one day in a rock pool. She thought it was the most beautiful thing she'd ever seen. Jason told her he would bring her plenty of combs if she would show him how to win a pearl.

"That's easy!" she told him. "You just have to win the dolphin race!" So Jason entered the dolphin race. But it was not as easy as he thought. He found that dolphins are very slippery to ride, and jumping through a hoop underwater is impossible. Unless, of course, you are a mermaid!

It was nearly time to go and Jason had not won a single prize! At the very last stall there was the biggest pearl he had ever seen. It was huge – almost as big as a coconut. The mermaids showed Jason what to do. He had to throw a sponge at the pearl to knock it over. Jason couldn't believe his luck! If there was one thing Jason could do, it was throw a sponge.

The mermaids gathered round to cheer him on.

He had one or two near misses and then, amidst lots of laughter, he knocked the huge pearl off the stand with his third try.

"You've won!" the mermaids shouted excitedly. "The pearl is yours!"

Jason swam back to his boat, delighted. The next day he returned clutching a box filled with pretty plastic combs. When the mermaids saw them they danced for joy in the waves and kissed him on both cheeks. After that Jason saw the mermaids whenever he went diving, and he always took them a special plastic comb.

The Clumsy FAIRY

Did you know that all fairies have to go to school to learn *how* to be fairies? Well they do! They have to learn how to fly, how to be graceful and how to do magic. Some fairies find it difficult. Clementine did!

Poor Clementine. She was the worst in the class. She was clumsy and awkward. When they were dancing she was the only fairy who tripped over her own feet.

"Clementine! Think of feathers, not elephants,"

Madame Bouquet, the fairy dance teacher, was forever saying.

At the end of term all the fairies were given a special task for the holidays. Sweetpea and Beatrice had to make garlands of flowers for the May Ball. Jemima and Poppy had to collect honey from the bees. Breeze and Scarlet had to polish the leaves on the holly tree.

But there was one task that no one wanted. This was to help a little girl who had measles.

"Clementine," said Madame Bouquet, "I want you to take this rose petal lotion, and paint it on the little girl's spots when she is asleep," said Madame Bouquet. "If you do this every night, for one whole week, the spots will disappear."

Clementine couldn't wait to start. That night she flew to the little girl's house and

in through the bedroom window. So far so good!
The little girl's name was Alice, and Clementine
could see her fast asleep in bed. She was holding a
fat, round teddy in her arms.

Clementine crept towards the bed. Then she
tripped over the rug and sat on a prickly hairbrush
which was lying on the floor.

"Ouch!" she yelled.

Alice stirred, but didn't wake. Clementine got up
quietly. She bent over to pick up the hairbrush, and a
toy clown, with a silly face, pinched her bottom!

"Ouch!" she yelled again.

This time Alice did wake up. "Who's there?" she
asked sleepily.

"It's Clementine," said the fairy, "and your clown just pinched my bottom!"

"Never did!" said the clown.

"Are you sure?" Alice asked Clementine, rubbing her eyes. "He's usually very well behaved."

Then Clementine overbalanced and sat down quickly on Alice's hot-water bottle which was lying on the floor. It was so bouncy that she shot straight up in the air and landed with a plop on Alice's bed.

"Are you alright?" asked Alice, rubbing her eyes again, to make sure she wasn't seeing things.

Clementine smoothed her crumpled dress and fluttered her wings. She explained to Alice why she had come.

"I'm sorry I woke you," she added. "You're not really supposed to see me."

Alice didn't mind. She thought it was lovely to be able to talk to a real fairy.

"Can you really do magic?" she asked Clementine. "Yes," Clementine told her. "I'm quite good at magic. I just wish I wasn't so clumsy."

She told Alice about her dance classes and Alice told Clementine about her ballet lessons.

"If you are helping me get rid of my measles," she said to Clementine, "I'll help you with your ballet."

So each night Clementine went to see Alice. Alice taught Clementine how to point her toes, how to keep her balance on one foot and how to curtsy gracefully. Clementine worked hard to copy everything Alice showed her. But it was the pirouette that Clementine did best of all. Holding her arms high above her head she twirled and twirled round Alice's bedroom.

In return, Clementine painted Alice's spots. Each day they became fainter and fainter. By the end of the week they had gone.

After the holidays the fairies went back to school.

"Now fairies," said Madame Bouquet, "I want you to show me *The Dance of the Sugar Plum Fairy.*"

The music started and the fairies began to dance. And, do you know, Clementine was the best dancer in the class. Madame Bouquet couldn't believe her eyes.

"Why, Clementine," she gasped, "you're my prima ballerina!"

And 'prima', as I'm sure you know, means 'first and best'!

Clementine was the happiest fairy in the world!

Sugarplum
- and the -
BUTTERFLY

Sugarplum," said the Fairy Queen, "I've got a very important job for you to do."

Sugarplum was always given the most important work. The Fairy Queen said it was because she was the kindest and most helpful of all the fairies.

"I want you to make a rose-petal ball gown for my birthday ball next week."

"It will be my pleasure," said Sugarplum happily. She liked being busy.

She set to work straight away. Sugarplum began to gather cobwebs to make the thread, and rose petals to make the dress. While she was collecting the thread she found a butterfly caught in a cobweb.

"Oh, you poor thing," sighed Sugarplum. She stopped what she was doing to help him. Very carefully, Sugarplum untangled the butterfly. But his wing was broken. Sugarplum laid the butterfly on a bed of feathers.

He was very sick and weak with hunger. Sugarplum gathered some nectar from a special flower and fed him a drop at a time. Then she set about mending his wing with a magic spell. Every day Sugarplum fed the butterfly with nectar and cast her spell to mend his wing. After six days, the butterfly was better. He was very grateful. But by now Sugarplum was behind with her work!

"I shall never finish the Fairy Queen's ball gown by tomorrow," she cried. "Whatever shall I do?"

The butterfly comforted her.

"Don't worry, Sugarplum," he said. "We will help you." He gathered all his friends together. There were yellow butterflies, blue butterflies, red and brown butterflies. He told them how Sugarplum had rescued him from the cobweb and helped to mend his wing. The butterflies gladly gathered up lots of rose petals and dropped them next to Sugarplum. Then the butterflies flew away to gather more cobwebs, while Sugarplum arranged all the petals.

Back and forth went Sugarplum's hand with her needle and thread making the finest cobweb stitches. Sugarplum added satin ribbons and bows. When she had finished, Sugarplum was very pleased.

"Dear friend," she said to the butterfly, "I couldn't have finished the dress without your help."

"And I couldn't have flown again without your kindness," said the butterfly.

The Fairy Queen was delighted with her new ball gown. And, when she heard the butterfly's story, she wrote a special 'Thank You' poem for Sugarplum:

Sugarplum is helpful,
Sugarplum is kind.
Sugarplum works hard all day,
But she doesn't mind.
She always does her very best,
To make sick creatures well.
She brings such joy and pleasure
As she weaves her magic spell!

The FOOTBALL Fairy

Georgina loved to play football. But there was just one problem.

"I'm fed up with these silly wings," she said, wiggling her shoulders. "They just get in the way."

The other fairies didn't agree at all.

"Whoever heard of a fairy without wings?" laughed Twinkletoes, doing a little dance.

"You wouldn't be able to fly if you didn't have wings," said Petal, landing on a flower.

"Flying is brilliant," called Sparkle, sprinkling fairy dust.

242

"Keep that fairy dust away from me," sneezed Georgina crossly. "I'm going to play football."

"Football is a game for elves, not fairies!" said Sparkle.

"In that case, I don't want to be a fairy!" said Georgina, and stamped off.

"She'll change her mind," said the wise fairy, "just wait and see."

But Georgina wouldn't change her mind. She pulled on her football boots and went to play with the elves.

The football game was very rough. The ball bounced around the field and, quite often, off the field! Sometimes it went up into the trees. Two birds who were trying to build their nest got very fed up, especially when the football landed near them.

Georgina flew up to get it. "Perhaps my wings can be useful after all," she thought, landing on the ground. She looked round quickly, hoping no one had seen her.

But someone had! Barry, the elf, was a tell-tale! He couldn't wait to tell the fairies what he had seen.

"Ah," nodded the wise fairy. "I knew she would use her wings sooner or later." But Georgina still wouldn't join in with the other fairies.

The next time she played football, the game was

rougher than ever. One elf kicked the ball so hard it flew into the tree and hit the birds' nest. This time there was an egg in it! The egg began to topple. None of the elves noticed; they were far too busy arguing with the referee. So Georgina flew up and, just in time, caught the egg before it hit the ground. Then she flew up to the nest.

"Thank you," said the mummy bird, rather sternly, tucking the egg back under her. "But please, in future, be more careful when you play football!"

Georgina promised she would.

When she flew down from the tree, Barry the tell-tale elf saw her. Of course, he told the fairies. They looked knowingly towards Georgina. "What did I tell you?" said the wise fairy. "She'll soon come round to being one of us."

Next time she played football, Georgina checked the tree first. The mummy bird was away. "Good!" she thought. "She can't complain this time." But, thanks to a naughty elf, the football knocked into the birds' nest. A small bundle of feathers tumbled out.

It was a baby bird!

Georgina spotted it and, quick as lightning, she flew up to catch him. Gently, she held him in her arms and flew back to the nest. When he was safely inside she sprinkled him with fairy dust to keep him from further harm. Just then mummy bird came back.

"I shall tell everyone about your kindness," she said, as her baby snuggled under her feathers. "And, as you're such a good fairy, will you be baby Beak's godmother?"

"I'd be delighted!" said Georgina.

When they heard the news, the other fairies were very proud of her.

"Perhaps it's not so bad being a fairy after all," grinned Georgina.

- The Tooth -
FAIRY

Pansy was nearly five. She couldn't wait for her birthday because Mum had promised her a party in the garden. There would be birthday cake and balloons and a funny clown. All her friends were coming to her party.

There was only one problem! Pansy's two front teeth were loose. They wobbled whenever she bit into anything. How was she going to enjoy her party food?

"Mum," she asked, for the

hundredth time, "will my wobbly teeth come out before my birthday party?"

"They'll come out when they're ready," said Mum, smiling.

That night Pansy woke suddenly. The curtains were open and her bed was covered in silvery moonlight. But that wasn't all! Sitting on Pansy's pillow was … can you guess? A fairy! It's true! She was tiny, with pale yellow wings, a wand and a sparkly dress.

Pansy could hardly believe it. She stared at the fairy, and the fairy stared back at her. The fairy spoke first.

"Can you see me?" she asked.

"Yes," said Pansy.

"That's funny," said the little fairy. "Usually I'm invisible!"

"Are you the tooth fairy?" asked Pansy.

"Yes, I'm Bobo," said the fairy. "I need two tiny front teeth to replace the keys on my piano."

Pansy showed Bobo her two front teeth. They were *very* wobbly.

"I hope they come out before my birthday party," said Pansy.

"They'll come out when they are ready," said Bobo. "If they come out before your birthday, I'll play my piano at your party!"

The next day, Bobo peeped into the playroom and found Pansy standing on her head!

"What are you doing, Pansy?" she asked.

"If I stay like this all day," said Pansy, "my teeth might fall out."

At teatime Bobo watched from behind a bowl of fruit, as Pansy ate all her cheese on toast, including the crusts. But still her teeth didn't come out!

"Try brushing your teeth," Bobo whispered to her, before Pansy went to bed.

"Oh yes! That will do it!" said Pansy. And she brushed and brushed and brushed, but the wobbly teeth just stayed stubbornly in her mouth.

The day before Pansy's birthday her two front teeth came out! It didn't hurt one little bit.

"Look!" she said to Mum, pulling a face, and showing a big gap where her teeth should be.

"Scary! Scary!" laughed Mum, pretending to be frightened.

"These are for Bobo," said Pansy, showing Mum the teeth.

"Who's Bobo?" asked Mum.

"The tooth fairy, of course," said Pansy.

That night Pansy went to bed early. She put her teeth under the pillow.

"I'll just close my eyes for a minute," she said to herself, "but I won't go to sleep."

Later Bobo came in, but Pansy had already dozed off. Bobo even whispered Pansy's name, but Pansy was fast asleep.

Pansy didn't wake until the sun shone through her curtains the next morning. The first thing she did was look under the pillow. The two tiny teeth had gone! In their place were two coins.

Pansy's fifth birthday party was the best she'd *ever* had. All her friends came. There was jelly and ice cream, balloons and the funniest clown she'd ever seen.

Her friends sang 'Happy Birthday' so loudly that Mum had to put her fingers in her ears. But only Pansy could hear the tiny fairy playing a piano and singing 'Happy Birthday' in a silvery voice.

The Yellow BLUEBELLS

The fairies at Corner Cottage were always busy. The garden was full of flowers and it was the fairies' job to look after them. You never saw them because they worked at night and hid during the day.

Blossom, the youngest fairy, was also one of

254

the busiest. It was her job to paint all the bluebells.

Corner Cottage had a lot of bluebells. They spread out under the apple tree like a deep blue carpet.

One evening, Blossom was sick.

"I've got a terrible cold," she told her friend Petal, sniffing loudly. "I don't think I can work tonight."

"I wish I could help," said Petal, "but I've got to spray the flowers with perfume or they won't smell right. You'll have to ask the gnomes."

Oh dear! Nobody liked asking Chip and Chuck, the garden gnomes. All they liked doing was fishing and windsurfing on the pond and playing tricks. Blossom was very worried about asking them.

"No problem!" said Chip and Chuck when she asked them. "Just leave it to us."

But Blossom was right to worry! When she got up the next morning the gnomes had painted some of the bluebells … YELLOW! She couldn't believe it.

"Have you seen what they've done?" she said to Petal. "What will Jamie think?"

Jamie lived in Corner Cottage with his mum and dad, and he played in the garden every day. That morning he came out as usual and made for the apple tree. It was a great tree for climbing. As he sat on his favourite branch, he looked down. Something looked different.

"I'm sure those flowers were blue yesterday," he thought.

"Mum," he said, going into the kitchen, "I've picked you some flowers."

"Yellowbells?" said Mum, putting them into a jam jar.

"Where did you get these?"

"Under the apple tree," said Jamie.

"How odd," said Mum. "I don't remember planting those."

That night, Blossom was still feeling ill.

"You'll have to paint the yellowbells again," she told the gnomes. But Chip and Chuck just chuckled.

In the morning, Jamie ran out to the garden and climbed the apple tree. This time the flowers were pink! He picked a bunch for his mum and she put them in the jam jar with the yellowbells.

When Petal told Blossom what had

257

happened, Blossom groaned. "I just knew something like this would happen." But she was still feeling too sick to work.

"Don't worry," said Petal. "Leave it to me." Petal made the naughty gnomes paint all the pinkbells again.

And this time she watched them carefully. The naughty gnomes grumbled loudly.

"Do it," said Petal, "or you'll never fish or windsurf on the pond again!"

The next morning, all the bluebells were blue again. Blossom was feeling much better.

"I'll be glad to get back to work!" she told Petal.

When Jamie and his mum went into the garden,

everything was as it should be. The bluebells were the right colour. And there was no sign of the yellowbells or pinkbells.

"It must have been the fairies!" joked Mum.

That night, as Jamie lay in bed he heard laughing and splashing from the fishpond. But, when Jamie peered through window, he couldn't see anything.

"Maybe it really was the fairies," he thought as he drifted off to sleep.

Misery the GRUMPY — Fairy —

Misery didn't have any friends. It was her own fault—she was always grumbling. She grumbled at the fairy who baked the bread. She grumbled at the fairy who mended her shoes. She even grumbled at the fairy who collected her honey. Willow, her niece, couldn't understand her.

"Why do you always find fault with everyone?" she asked.

"Because everybody is so useless," said her grumpy aunt.

One day Misery told the
fairy who baked the bread,
"Your bread is too soft. I
like crusty bread."

"If that's your attitude,"
said the baker fairy, "you
can bake your own bread."

"I shall!" said Misery.

The next day she was rude to the
fairy who mended her shoes.

"No one speaks to me like that!" said the cobbler
fairy. "From now on you can
mend your own shoes."

"I'll be glad to," said
Misery grumpily.

Then she insulted the
fairy who collected the
honey from the honeybees.

"How dare you?" said the
fairy. "I'm not staying here to be

insulted. You can collect your own honey." And she stormed off.

Soon there was no one in the village who would do anything for Misery.

"You've been rude to everyone," said Willow. "How are you going to manage?"

"No problem," said Misery. "I shall do everything myself."

She set to work the very next day to bake some bread. First she lit a fire to get the oven really hot. Then she made some dough and mixed and kneaded it until her arms ached. Then she left the dough to

rise. She put the loaf in the oven, and sat down for a well-earned rest.

Of course, she fell asleep! A smell of burning woke her! Rushing to the oven she flung open the door. All that was left of the loaf of bread were a few burnt cinders.

But what Misery didn't realise was that the baker fairy didn't bake bread in the usual way. No! She used a special baking spell – a spell that Misery didn't know!

Misery was still determined to carry on. She went to collect some honey from the bees. She watched them buzzing round the hive. Misery just waved her arms at them, shouting, "Out of my way, bees."

They didn't like it one little bit!

Their answer was to swarm around her and sting her nose and chin. You see, what Misery didn't know was that the honey fairy used the special honey-collecting spell.

Misery ran from the bees as fast as she could and, as she did, she lost her shoe!

Oh dear! What a state she was in! Burnt bread, bee stings on her nose and chin, and only one shoe!

"You can't go on like this," said Willow, when she saw her.

Misery did some serious thinking.

"Tell all the fairies I've turned over a new leaf," she told Willow. "From now on I shan't be a grumpy fairy any more."

Willow was delighted! So were the other fairies. Misery threw a large party as a way of saying sorry. Misery didn't complain about anything for months after that, and Willow kept her fingers crossed that it would last!

The ENCHANTED Garden

Princess Sylvie grew up in a beautiful castle, but it had no garden. So she loved to walk through the meadows just to look at the flowers. Princess Sylvie loved flowers!

One day Princess Sylvie found an overgrown path. She asked a woman where the path led.

"That path leads to the garden of the enchantress!" said the woman.

"What is an enchantress?" Princess Sylvie asked.

"Someone who uses magic! So be warned … don't pick the flowers or who knows what terrible things might happen!"

Princess Sylvie followed the path until she came to a small cottage with the prettiest garden she had ever seen! It was filled with flowers of every colour and perfume!

After that, Princess Sylvie went every day. Winter came and snow lay thick, yet the garden stayed the same.

Princess Sylvie forgot all about the enchantress. One wintry day, she picked a rose from the garden and took it back to the castle. As she put it in water, Princess Sylvie suddenly remembered the warning! She'd picked a flower from the enchanted garden and who knew what terrible things might happen?

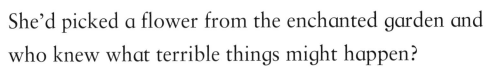

But days passed and nothing happened. The rose stayed as fresh as the day it was picked. Then months passed and still nothing happened. Forgetting her fears, Princess Sylvie decided to go back to the enchanted garden.

When she saw the garden, Princess Sylvie wanted to cry! The grass was brown. The flowers had withered and died! Then she heard someone weeping. Inside the cottage the enchantress was sitting by the fire, crying. She was old and bent. Although Princess Sylvie was afraid, she felt sorry for her.

"What happened to your lovely garden?" Princess Sylvie asked.

"Someone picked a rose from my magic garden!" said the enchantress. "The rose will live forever, but the rest must die!"

"Can't your magic bring the garden back to life?"

Princess Sylvie asked.

"Alas, when the rose
was picked, my magic
was lost! And now,
I too will wither
and die!"

"What can I do?"
asked Princess Sylvie,
heartbroken.

"Only a princess
can bring my magic back,"
she replied.

"How?" asked Princess Sylvie.

"She must bring me six sacks of stinging nettles!
No princess would do such a thing."

Princess Sylvie didn't say anything. She turned
and ran to the meadow. She gathered up armful after
armful of nettles, not caring that they stung her. She
filled six sacks and took them back to the
enchantress.

"You are kind," she said. "But the nettles must be picked by a princess."

"But I am a princess," said Princess Sylvie.

Without delay, the enchantress made a magic potion with the nettles and drank it. Instantly, the garden became enchanted again! Princess Sylvie gasped! Gone was the bent old lady and in her place was a beautiful young woman.

"My beautiful garden is restored," smiled the enchantress, "and so am I!"

And so the enchantress and the princess became great friends and shared the enchanted garden.

— Princess —
ROSEBUD

In a beautiful palace in a land far away, lived a little princess. The king and queen called her Princess Rosebud, because on her left ankle was a small pink mark in the shape of a rose.

On her third birthday, Princess Rosebud was given a pretty white pony. The princess rode her pony with her nanny and her groom at her side. They went to the edge of the forest then stopped for a rest. The pretty white pony was tied to a tree branch. The nanny and the groom talked

together, while the little princess wandered along a forest path collecting flowers and leaves. They didn't notice how far the little princess had wandered. Soon Princess Rosebud couldn't see her nanny or her groom or her beautiful white pony. She called and called for her nanny. But no one came. It began to get dark. The little princess was scared and began to cry.

Princess Rosebud walked on until she saw a light through the trees. There was a little house with a straw roof and tiny little windows and a small wooden door. Suddenly, the door opened. There stood a little old woman!

Now, the old woman was blind and couldn't see the little princess, but she could hear a small child crying. The old woman was kind. She took the little princess inside and sat her by a warm fire. Then she gave her thin slices of bread and honey, and a glass of milk.

"What is your name, child?" she asked.

"Rosebud," answered the princess.

"Where do you live, child?" she asked.

"I don't know," answered the princess. "I got lost in the forest."

"Well, you can stay with me until someone comes to find you, my dear," said the kind old woman.

Back at the palace, the king and queen were very upset that their only daughter was lost. They offered a reward of a hundred gold coins to anyone who

could find her. But many years went by and no one found the little princess. The king and queen thought they would never see the princess again.

Meanwhile Rosebud was very happy living in the forest. She forgot that she had ever been a princess! She forgot she had lived in a palace! She forgot her fine clothes and jewels. She even forgot her white pony!

One day, when she was walking in the garden, a pony galloped into view. He was as white as milk, and had a jewelled saddle and bridle!

Rosebud loved him immediately! She climbed into the saddle, and the pony turned swiftly, and galloped off! He took her to the palace gate. Rosebud felt she had seen the palace before, but could not remember when. Before dark, the pony returned her to the cottage in the forest.

The next day he came again, and again they visited the palace before returning to the cottage.

Then the next day, the palace gate was open. The pony trotted through the gate just as the king and queen were walking in the gardens. They saw the little girl and the pony and thought she was the prettiest girl they had ever seen.

"What is your name, child?" the queen asked her.

"Rosebud, your majesty," Rosebud replied.

"Ah," sighed the queen sadly, "that is the name of my long-lost daughter."

Then, just as Rosebud was mounting the pony to ride home, the queen noticed the pink rose on her left ankle!

She stared at it in disbelief!

"Sire!" she cried to the king. "It is our daughter, Princess Rosebud."

The whole kingdom rejoiced to hear that the princess had returned. The king offered the old woman a reward for caring for the princess, but she shook her head.

"I only want to be near Rosebud for the rest of my days," she said. And so the old woman came to live in the palace with Princess Rosebud.

The Pig and

THE JEWELS

Daisy was as pretty as a picture. She was very kind too. Daisy looked after all the animals on the farm where she lived. She loved them all dearly, and the animals all loved her too.

But Daisy dreamt of being more than a farmer's daughter. As she fed the hens and the ducks or counted the sheep, Daisy day-dreamed about being a princess. At night when she lay in bed she would say to herself, "Oh, how I wish I could be a princess!"

One day she found a sick pig

at the edge of the forest. She carried him to the farm and nursed him until he was better. The pig became her favourite animal, and he followed her wherever she went.

She told him all her secrets, and he listened carefully, his little eyes fixed on hers. It was almost as if he understood everything she said. She even told him the most important secret of all.

"Dear little pig," she whispered in his ear, " I wish, I wish I could be a princess!"

That night the pig went away. When he returned the next morning, he had a tiara made of precious jewels on his head. The pig stood in front of Daisy, the jewels glinting in the sunshine.

"Darling pig," cried Daisy, "is that for me?"

The pig grunted. Daisy took the tiara and put it on her head. It fitted her perfectly.

The next night the pig went away again. In the morning he returned as before, this time with a beautiful necklace. Daisy put it on.

"How do I look?" she asked him. But of course the pig just grunted.

After that the pig went away every night for six nights. And every morning for six mornings he returned with something different.

First he brought a dress of white silk, followed by

a crimson cloak and soft leather shoes. Then bracelets set with jewels, and long lengths of satin ribbon for her hair. And, finally, a ring made of gold and rubies.

Daisy put on all the gifts the pig had brought her and stood in front of a long mirror.

"At last," she whispered to her reflection, "I look just like a real princess."

The next day the pig disappeared again. Daisy didn't worry because she knew he always returned. But days went by and then weeks, and the pig did not return. Daisy missed him more than she could say.

Summer turned to autumn, and autumn to winter. The days grew short and snow lay in deep drifts on the ground. Daisy spent the evenings sitting by the fire in her white silk dress and crimson cloak. Her heart was sad and heavy when she thought about her dear, lost pig.

"I would be happy just to remain a farmer's daughter if only he would return to me," she cried, watching the logs burn in the hearth.

Suddenly there was a noise at the door – it was the pig! With a cry of joy she bent to kiss him and, as she did, he turned into a handsome prince!

Daisy gasped with amazement.

"Sweet Daisy," said the prince taking her hand. "If it wasn't for you I would still be alone and friendless, wandering in the forest."

He explained how a wicked witch had cast a spell on him to turn him into a pig. "Your kiss broke the spell," said the prince. "Daisy, will you marry me?"

It was a dream come true. At long last, Daisy really was going to become Princess Daisy!

— The — PRINCESS Who Never Smiled

A long time ago, in a far-off land, a princess was born. The king and queen called her Princess Columbine. They thought she was the most precious child ever to be born. And, to make sure that she was watched over every minute of every day, they hired a nurse to look after her.

One day, the queen came to the nursery and found the nurse asleep and the little princess crying. The queen was very cross and called for the king. He told off the nurse for not watching the baby.

But what the king and queen didn't know was that the nurse was really a wicked enchantress. The angry enchantress cast a spell over the little baby princess:

"Princess Columbine will never smile again until she learns my real name!"

The king and queen were devastated. From that day on, the princess never smiled! Names were collected from all over the land. They tried all the usual names such as Jane, Catherine, Amanda. They tried more unusual names such as Araminta, Tallulah, Leanora. They even tried quite outlandish names such as Dorominty, Truditta, Charlottamina. But none broke the spell.

Princess Columbine grew up to be a sweet and beautiful girl. Everybody loved her. But her face was always so sad, it made the king and queen unhappy. They tried everything to make her smile. They bought her a puppy. They even hired a court jester who told the silliest jokes you've ever heard.

"Why did the pecans cross the road?" asked the jolly jester. The princess shrugged.

"Because they were nuts!" the jester laughed.

"Why did the ice-cream?" the jester tried again. The princess just gazed politely.

"Because the jelly wobbled!"

One day an artist called Rudolpho came to the palace and asked the king if he could paint the princess's portrait. The king agreed on one condition.

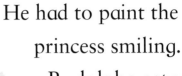

He had to paint the princess smiling. Rudolpho set up his easel beneath a large mirror and began straight away. The princess sat opposite watching him paint in the mirror behind him. As he worked, Rudolpho asked the princess about all the people in the palace. He had soon painted the princess's portrait, all except for her smile. But he couldn't make the princess smile.

Rudolpho tried some funny drawings. He drew silly pictures of the king and queen. The princess looked on politely. Then he drew a picture of her old nurse and gave her a moustache, and above he wrote NURSE. Princess Columbine gazed in the mirror. There, above the picture, was the word NURSE spelled out back to front – ƎƧЯUИ.

"ESRUN," Princess Columbine said quietly. And then she smiled. "Her name is ESRUN!" laughed Princess Columbine. At last the spell was broken! The king and queen heard her laughter and came rushing to see what was happening. They were so happy that soon everyone in the palace was laughing too.

The Tale of Two
PRINCESSES

Long ago there were twin princesses called Charmina and Charlotte. Even though they were twins, the princesses were very different. In fact they were opposites. Princess Charmina was gracious and charming to everyone. She curtsied politely to the king and queen. And she stood quite still while the royal dressmakers came to fit her new ball gown.

Princess Charlotte was very different!

"Why do I have to dress like a puffball?" grumbled Princess Charlotte when it was her turn to have a new ball gown fitted.

"How dare you speak to us like that!" her parents cried.

But she did dare. She dared to run barefoot through the gardens until her hair looked like a bush. She dared to wear her shabbiest clothes. In fact, she didn't behave like a princess at all!

One day there was to be a ball at the palace. The guests of honour were two princes from the next kingdom. The two princesses, dressed in their new ball gowns, kept getting in the way of the preparations. "Why don't you go for a walk until our guests arrive?" suggested the queen. "But stay together, don't get dirty and don't be late!"

The two princesses walked to the bottom of the palace gardens.

"Let's go into the forest," said Princess Charlotte to her sister.

"I don't think we should," said Princess Charmina. "Our gowns will get dirty." But Princess Charlotte had already set off.

"Wait for me!" called Princess Charmina. "We must stay together!" They wandered deeper and deeper into the forest. They crunched through fallen leaves, listening to the birds singing.

"I think we should go back," Princess Charmina told her sister. "We'll be late for the ball."

Just then they heard a strange noise.

"Let's turn back!" said Princess Charmina, afraid.

"It may be someone in distress!" said Princess Charlotte. "We must go and help!"

Although Princess Charmina was scared, she agreed. "But we must get back in time for the ball."

"Don't worry, we will," said Princess Charlotte.

They set off again going even deeper into the forest. Finally, they came upon two horses in a clearing, but there was no sign of their riders. Just then they heard voices calling out,

"Who's there?"

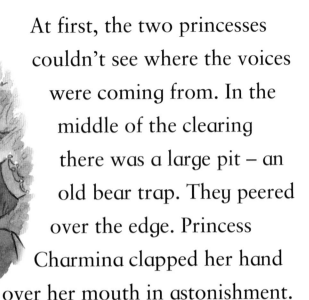

At first, the two princesses couldn't see where the voices were coming from. In the middle of the clearing there was a large pit – an old bear trap. They peered over the edge. Princess Charmina clapped her hand over her mouth in astonishment.

Princess Charlotte burst out laughing. There at the bottom of the pit were two princes.

"How do you do?" said the first prince.

"Well, don't just stand there," said the second prince. "Help us out!"

The two princesses found ropes and threw one end down to the princes. They tied the other end to their horses.

Soon the princes were rescued and laughed with the princesses. They all set off to the palace together.

On their return they found everyone in the palace in a state of panic. The king and queen were angry when their daughters returned late looking so dirty. But their anger turned to joy when the two princes explained what had happened.

Everyone enjoyed the ball. The two princesses danced all night with the two princes. And, do you know, from that time on, Charlotte paid more attention to her gowns and hair. And Charmina became a little more playful and daring than before!

The Princess of HEARTS

Princess Ruby was given her name because she was born with ruby-red lips the shape of a tiny heart. When she grew up she was very beautiful, with coal-black hair down to her waist, green eyes and skin as pale as milk.

She was a charming and friendly girl, but she insisted that everything she owned was heart-shaped! Her bed was heart-shaped, her table and chair were heart-shaped, her cushions were heart-shaped, even the

sandwiches her maid brought her at tea time were cut into the shape of hearts!

As soon as she was old enough, the king and queen wanted Princess Ruby to find a husband.

"There is a prince in the next kingdom who is looking for a wife," they told her. "He is brave and handsome and rich. Everything a princess could wish for."

But the foolish princess declared: "I will only marry this prince if he can change the stars in the sky to hearts!"

The king and queen didn't know how to answer!

When Prince Gallant came to visit he was indeed as handsome as her parents had said. Princess Ruby liked his kindly eyes and his pleasant smile.

They spent the afternoon walking in the palace

gardens, and talking about everything under the sun. But Prince Gallant could not promise Princess Ruby that he could change the shape of the stars. So the princess could not marry him!

As she watched the prince ride away, Princess Ruby suddenly wished she had not been so foolish!

Prince Gallant was unhappy, too, as he rode home through the forest. Suddenly, he heard a screeching sound. In the clearing, a dragon was attacking a peacock. Jumping off his horse, the prince took out his sword and chased the dragon away. The peacock was in a sorry state. All his beautiful tail feathers were scattered around him.

"Thank you for saving me," said the peacock. The prince was astonished to hear the peacock talk. "I have magical powers," explained the peacock. "But I am now very weak. The dragon has pulled out some of my magic feathers!"

The prince set to work gathering up all the peacock's feathers. As soon as the feathers had been returned, the peacock gave a loud cry and spread his tail wide. The peacock's tail glowed.

"Before I go, I will grant you a single wish," he told the prince. Prince Gallant wished that the stars in the sky would change into the shape of hearts!

Later that night Princess Ruby was sitting in her bedchamber. Now she was really regretting that she had refused to marry Prince Gallant.

Feeling sad she looked out of the window at the full moon casting its radiant light over the hills and fields beyond the palace.

Then she glanced at the stars – and couldn't believe her eyes!

Every single one was in the shape of a silver heart!

At that moment she saw Prince Gallant riding over the hill. He stopped his horse beneath Princess Ruby's window.

She was overjoyed to see him.

"Will you ever forgive me," she cried, "for being so foolish as to ask you to change the shape of the stars?"

"There is nothing to forgive," said the prince, and again he asked if she would marry him. Filled with delight Princess Ruby, of course, agreed!

They were married on a lovely summer's day. And when Princess Ruby made her wedding vows, she promised never to ask for anything foolish again!

—Sports—
DAY

The sun peeped over the higgledy-piggledy, messy alley. It was much too early to be awake – or was it?

Lenny the kitten slowly opened his eyes and grinned – it was time-to-get-up time.

"Get up, Sleepyhead!" he yelled to his twin sister, Lulu. "It's a great day for running and jumping." And he started to run round and round the dustbins.

"OK, Lenny," yawned Lulu, still half asleep, "I'm coming."

"Let's have some fun!" cried Lenny. "What about some jumping?"

So, huffing and puffing, the little kittens piled up some boxes and put a pole across the gap.

Lenny leapt over it first. "Whee!" he cried. "I bet I can jump higher than you!"

Suddenly, Lulu spotted a tatty old ball.

"I bet I can throw it further than you!" she cried.

"No, you can't," cried Lenny. He picked up the ball and

threw his best throw ever – but it hit Uncle Bertie right on the head!

Scampering down the alley as fast as they could go, the two kittens quickly hid behind a heap of old potato sacks before Uncle Bertie could spot them!

"Pooh!" said Lulu. "These sacks are smelly!"

Suddenly, Lenny had an idea... Standing in a potato sack and pulling it up to his tummy, he began hopping and jumping around!

Lenny hopped and skipped while Lulu wiggled and giggled as they raced each other.

"I'm winning!" squealed Lulu. "I'm winning!"

"No, you're not!" cried Lenny. He jumped his best jump ever – and knocked a huge pile of boxes over Cousin Archie!

"Uh-oh!" groaned Lenny. "Trouble time!"

Uncle Bertie and Cousin Archie were not happy. They stomped off to find Hattie, the kittens' mother.

"Those kittens of yours are *so* naughty," they complained. "You've got to do something about them!"

Hattie sighed. Then, spying two pairs of tiny ears peeping out from behind a watering can, she tip-toed over. "Time-to-come-out time!" she boomed.

But Hattie wasn't cross. She knew her kittens were only playing. "I've got an idea," she said. "Why don't we have a sports day? Then there'll be plenty of running and jumping for everyone!" Later that day, Hattie explained her idea to the Alley Dogs, who all thought it sounded like great fun. It wasn't long before Hattie had organised everyone and everything!

"We'll have lots of different races," cried Lenny excitedly, "running, skipping, hopping, leaping and jumping ones – maybe even a sack race!"

"OK, everyone," cried Hattie. "Let's begin. Ready… steady… "

"Er, Hattie," asked Cousin Archie, popping out from behind the fence, "can I join in?"

"Us too?" cried Uncle Bertie and Auntie Lucy.

"Of course you can," laughed Hattie.

"Ready... steady... GO!"

Cousin Archie and Uncle Bertie raced up the alley and passed the winning line together. "Archie and Bertie are the winners!" cried Hattie. "Time for the sack race now!"

They all climbed into their sacks. But Lenny and Lulu began before Hattie could say "Go!"

"Hey!" cried Hattie, "come back you two, that's cheating!" But it was too late. Everyone began leaping and jumping after the kittens.

"STOP!" shouted Hattie. And Lenny and Lulu stopped – but no one else did! They crashed into each other and fell in a big Alley Dog and Cat pickle!

No one was hurt, but they were all tired.

"That was the best sports day ever!" said Harvey.

Hattie looked at the higgledy-piggledy mess.

"You are right," she laughed. "But tomorrow we're going to play another game. It's called tidy up the alley!"

"Oh, no!" they groaned, and lots of barking and meowing filled the air... and then they all laughed.

—Birthday— SURPRISE

In the higgledy-piggledy, messy alley, the sun was just beginning to shine. It was very early. Even the birds hadn't begun to chirp and cheep yet. Everyone was fast asleep. Or were they?

Slowly, a sleepy head peeped out of a dustbin. It was Uncle Bertie.

First he opened one eye... then the other... and gave a great big grin!

"It's here, at last!" he chuckled to himself.

"Happy Birthday to me! Happy Birthday to me!"

he sang, at the top of his voice. He looked around, but no one had heard. Everyone was still snoozing and snoring! Didn't they know it was his birthday?

"Time-to-get-up time!" he shouted, as he banged on a dustbin lid – CLANG! CLANG! CLANG!

Lenny and Lulu, the two kittens, fell out of their basket in fright. Cousin Archie tumbled off his branch, right on top of poor Hattie!

"Uncle Bertie!" snapped Hattie, the kittens' mother, "why are you bashing that dustbin lid?"

"Sorry!" said Uncle Bertie. "Er... it's just that it's my... er... well, it's time-to-get-up time!"

"Oh, Bertie!" sighed Hattie. Now she was awake, she decided to get up and get her kittens ready. How they wriggled and wiggled – they hated wash time!

Cousin Archie scritched and scratched his claws on an old mat. Auntie Lucy just rolled over and went back to sleep! Poor Uncle Bertie! How sad he looked. Wasn't anyone going to wish him a happy birthday?

Then Bertie spotted the twins chasing a butterfly.

"Hey, you two!" he called. "Bet you don't know what day it is today."

"Of course we do," said Lulu. "It's Saturday!"

"It's not, Loony Lulu!" said Lenny, pushing his sister into a puddle!

"No, twins," said Uncle Bertie, "it's my— "

But the naughty kittens had already run away.

Suddenly, Archie jumped out from behind a box.

"Hello, Cousin Archie," said Bertie. "Bet you don't know what today is!"

"I'm not telling!" giggled Archie, and scampered off down the alley. "It's for me to know and you to find out!"

"But I know!" cried Bertie. "It's my *birthday*!"

But Archie was already gone.

"I know who will remember!" said Bertie. "Harvey, the Alley Dog will – he knows everything!" And he rushed up the alley to find him.

"Hello, guys," called Bertie to the dogs. "Guess what today is?"

"Nosh day?" rumbled Ruffles, the Old English Sheepdog.

"No!" meowed Bertie, crossly. "Doesn't anyone know? It's—"

"Chasing Bertie day!" barked Harvey and started to run after him.

Bertie ran down the alley and jumped over the fence into the apple orchard.

"I don't care anyway!" he sulked.

"Who wants a rotten old birthday?"

Poor Bertie didn't see the five pairs of cats' eyes peeping over the fence. And he didn't hear five pussies, planning and giggling!

"This is the worst birthday ever!" wailed Bertie.

"Tee-hee," whispered Cousin Archie. "Looks as though our plan is working!"

"I need to find the Alley Dogs," purred Hattie and clambered down from the fence. Luckily, Harvey was already there!

"Is everything ready?" she asked.

Harvey smiled and nodded his head.

Back in the orchard, Uncle Bertie was fed up.
He decided to go home and have a sleep. He squeezed
through the tiny gap in the fence.

"SURPRISE!" yelled the Alley Cats and Dogs.
The alley was decorated with bright, colourful
streamers. There was even a cake in the shape of a
fish! Bertie was so happy!

"You remembered!" said Bertie.

"Oh, Bertie," said Hattie, "how could we
forget!" She gave him a big hug.

"Thanks, gang!" grinned Bertie. "This is the best
birthday ever!"

— Little —
LOST LENNY

One grey day, Lenny the kitten was happily chasing his twin sister, Lulu, around the higgledy-piggledy, messy alley. They were having great fun, leaping over boxes and through tyres.

Hattie, their mummy, looked up at the big, dark clouds. "I think it's going to rain," she said. "Come on, everyone, let's put everything away."

Everyone was busy helping... or were they? Lenny was planning something! He snatched Lulu's teddy

and with a giggle, ran off down the alley. Lulu gave a long wail. Teddy was her favourite toy.

Lenny stopped at the bottom of the alley and called to his sister. "Come and get Teddy!"

As Lulu raced down the alley, Lenny tossed the teddy high into the sky. He went straight over his sister's head and disappeared behind a large fence! Lenny knew he was going to be in big trouble.

Little Lulu sobbed and told her mummy what her naughty brother had done.

Everyone looked at Lenny.

"Lenny, you really are a naughty pussy!" said his mother, crossly. "You know you're not supposed to come down to this part of the alley."

"Please don't worry, Lulu," Bertie said, kindly.

"Archie and I will find Teddy for you later."
Lenny stood still, bit his lip and trembled.
"Why do you have to get into so much
trouble?" asked Hattie.
"And why can't you
be more helpful like
your sister?"
"Sorry, Mummy,"
whispered Lenny, and
a big, fat tear trickled down his cheek.

"It's not fair," he thought. "I didn't mean to lose
silly old Teddy!"

Lenny gave a sniff and wandered over to the
gate. He peeped through the bars. Mummy had said
that they must never, ever go through this gate.

"But I don't know why," thought Lenny. "I do
know that Teddy's in there, though," he said, "and
I must try and get him back." So he squeezed himself
through the bars...

Lenny found himself standing at the edge of a big

building site. There were lots of wooden planks and piles of bricks – Lenny thought it looked great fun.

"I don't know why Mummy told me to keep away from here," he laughed. "It's like having my very own adventure playground."

The naughty pussy soon forgot about feeling sad as he climbed ladders and walked across gangplanks, high above the ground, even though it was raining.

"I'm Lucky Lenny the Pirate!" he laughed. Then he stopped and peered through the rain. "And there's Teddy!" he cried.

As Lenny grabbed the bear, the plank tipped up. The rain had made it very slippery

and... down, down, down he fell – all the way to the bottom of a mucky, muddy hole.

Luckily, cats always land on their feet, so he wasn't hurt, but he'd had a real fright! And now he was stuck! "Mummy! Mummy!" he meowed.

Meanwhile, Hattie looked round the alley. "Where's Lenny?" she asked the others. But no one had seen him for ages.

"Go and get the dogs," she said to Archie. "Ask them to help us find my poor little Lenny."

Archie quickly returned with Harvey and the gang. "Don't worry, Hattie," said Harvey. "We'll soon find him for you."

All the dogs and cats ran out into the pouring rain, meowing and barking Lenny's name. At the bottom of the alley, the Old English Sheepdog, Ruffles, snuffled at the gate. "Yes, he's in there!" cried Patchy, the dog with a patch over one eye, "I can hear him crying!"

"Don't worry!" called Harvey. "We'll soon get you out."

Ruffles, Harvey and Bertie lowered a thick rope to Lenny. The tiny kitten clung on tight and was pulled to safety.

Lenny gave Teddy back to Lulu. "I didn't mean to make you sad," he said.

"We were so worried!" said Hattie. "No special kitty treats for you tonight."

"I'm really sorry, Mummy," sniffed Lenny.

Hattie smiled and gave her naughty, little kitten a big hug. "That's OK," she smiled. "At least you're safe now."

Then, all the Alley Cats went back to the alley for lots of cat napping!

— Fire! —

FIRE!

The sun was shining in the higgledy-piggledy, messy alley.

"It's much too hot!" Hattie thought to herself, as she tried to find a nice shady spot for a snooze. Everyone was hiding from the sun – everyone except Cousin Archie! Archie didn't notice the sun's rays shining through the glass of

those empty milk bottles. It was focused right on to Hattie's dustbin full of old newspapers – the perfect place for a fire to start!

Suddenly, Hattie's nose twitched. "What's that?" she wondered. "It smells like smoke. It *is* smoke!" she gasped, as she saw bright red and yellow flames leaping out of her dustbin. "F-Fire! Help! Wake up, Bertie!" cried Hattie. "My dustbin's on fire!"

Uncle Bertie's sleepy head popped up from his dustbin.

"I must have been dreaming, Hattie!" he yawned. "I dreamt that your bin was on fire."

"It wasn't a dream," cried Hattie. "My bin *is* on fire."

All the shouting woke the twins from their dreams. "Mummy! Mummy!" they meaowed, "what's happening?"

Hattie grabbed her kittens and put them on the top of the fence, well away from the dangerous fire.

"Hooray!" cried Bertie, finding a bucket half full of water. "It might be enough to put out the fire."

"Cousin Archie!" he cried. "Come and help me."

The two cats ran down the alley, carrying the bucket between them. Then Archie and Bertie aimed the bucket of water and let go... SPLOSH! There was a huge sizzling sound.

"Hooray!" Bertie cried, sounding relieved. "We've done it!"

But suddenly, they noticed that a spark from the fire had landed on the rubbish next to the dustbin.

"Oh no!" wailed Archie. "The rubbish is on fire! Help!" he shrieked, as he hurtled down the alley to the dogs, who were all fast asleep. "Hattie's bin is on fire. It's spreading down the alley and we can't put it out."

But no one stirred. Archie was always playing tricks on the Alley Dogs and today it was just too hot to bother.

Harvey opened one eye lazily. "That's a good one, Archie!" he said.

"It's true!" Archie shouted, desperately. "Look!"

"This had better not be one of your tricks, Archie," Harvey growled. Then he shaded his eyes from the sun and looked up the alley.

As soon as he saw the billowing smoke, he knew the Alley Cat was telling the truth.

"Archie's right!" barked Harvey. "Quick, everyone to the rescue!"

The dogs raced up the alley towards the fire.

The alley was filled with smelly black smoke.

All the cats were coughing and choking. But Harvey knew just what to do.

"Quick!" he said. "Everybody to the water barrel. Use anything you can to collect the water."

Grabbing old buckets and cans, the cats and dogs formed a long line. Auntie Lucy stood by the barrel to fill up the containers. Then, splishing and splashing, they passed the water along the line to Harvey, who threw it over the fire.

Suddenly, Lucy gave a cry. "The water's run out!"

"Oh no!" said Archie. "We'll *never* put the fire out now."

The Alley Cats and Dogs stared in dismay. What could they do? They must have more water.

"I know what to do," coughed Lenny. Grabbing his sister and Puddles, he pulled them over the fence. "I've just remembered what's in this garden."

When he came back, he was pulling a hose.

Harvey grabbed the nozzle, as Bertie leapt over the fence and raced to turn the tap on.

With a mighty spurt, the water sploshed out, drenching everything. Everyone cheered! Some of the water splashed over the cats and dogs – but they didn't care. The fizzling, sizzling fire was out!

"You little ones deserve a treat for saving our alley!" barked Harvey. "Puppy snacks for you, Puddles and kitty nibbles for the twins."

"Three cheers for Lenny, Lulu and Puddles!" cried Archie. "Hip-hip-hooray!"

—Barking—
NIGHT

It was the middle of the night in the higgledy-piggledy, messy alley. Everyone and everything was fast asleep – or were they?

Six naughty alley cats peeped over the fence. They spied the snoozing dogs and, grinning and sniggering, they scrabbled up the fence.

"I've got an idea!" whispered Archie. "Listen..."

Wibbling and wobbling, the alley cats stood in a line along the top of the fence...

"Those dippy dogs are in for a fright!" giggled Archie.

"I bet I'll be the loudest!" boasted Lenny.

The cats took a deep breath, and out came the scariest, screechiest sounds you ever did hear!

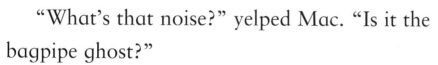

The terrible noise woke Harvey with a start and made him fall off his mattress, straight on to Mac!

"What's that noise?" yelped Mac. "Is it the bagpipe ghost?"

"G-Ghost?" cried a frightened Puddles. "Help!"

The noise made Patchy and Ruffles jump. They fell in a big heap on top of Ruffles' bed! "Save us!" they cried.

Harvey spotted the culprits. "Oh, it's just those pesky pussies," he groaned, "up to mischief as usual. Don't worry, everyone, let's just ignore them and go back to sleep."

But those naughty cats weren't finished yet!

"Louder! Louder!" screeched Archie to the others. But could they wake Bonnie? Oh no! She just kept on snoring and snoring and snoring!

"Someone should teach those cats a lesson," growled Mac. "When I was a pup I'd..."

"*Not now, Mac,*" shouted the others.

Harvey smiled. He had a good idea. The gang huddled together and listened.

The cats thought they were so clever. They laughed and wailed even louder! Then suddenly, Lenny slipped and grabbed Lulu, who grabbed Hattie, who grabbed Bertie, who grabbed Lucy, who grabbed Archie – and they all tumbled headfirst into the pile of boxes and bins!

"Bravo!" woofed the dogs. "More! More!"

The cats squealed and wailed and ran away. They'd had enough of playing tricks for one day!

"Now to get our own back," chuckled Harvey.

The gang sneaked along the alley as quiet as little mice.

"Ready?" whispered Harvey. "Steady – GO!"

"WOOF! WOOF!"

The ground shook and the cats jumped high into the air.

"Ha-ha!" roared the dogs. "Scaredy-cats! Scaredy-cats! We've got our own back!"

"I think that's enough frights for one night!" said Harvey.

"You're right," agreed Archie, sheepishly. "Let's all go back to bed. No more tricks tonight."

Just then Bonnie woke up. "Is it time-to-get-up time?" she asked, rubbing her eyes.

"No!" said Patchy, "it's time-for-bed time!" and they all laughed and laughed.

"Oh, goody!" yawned Bonnie. "Bedtime! The best time of the day!"

"Oh, Bonnie," smiled Harvey. "What a sleepyhead you are! How could you sleep through all that noise?"

But Bonnie didn't care. With another enormous yawn and a stretch, she turned away and wandered back to her dustbin – she was soooo tired!

At last the cats and dogs of the higgledy-piggledy, messy alley snuggled down to sleep, dreaming of chasing dustbin men – and yummy bones and bowls of scrummy fish! The only sounds were the rumblings of Ruffles' tummy and Bonnie's snores.

Everyone and everything was fast asleep – or were they?

"TOOWHIT– TOOWHOO!"

—Troublesome—
SISTER

In the higgledy-piggledy, messy alley it was tidy-up time! Harvey and the gang worked hard to clean up their home until, at last, the skip was full of rubbish. The gang settled down for a snooze, except for Puddles, Harvey's sister.

"Where's my teddy? And my ish?" she asked. Puddles' ish was a blanket she'd had since she was a puppy. She looked round the alley.

"Teddy! Ish!" she called. "Where are you?" She didn't see them peeping out from the top of the skip.

Puddles was always getting into lots of mischief and today she scampered off down the alley, sure that she would find her teddy and ish down there somewhere. Squeezing through a hole in the fence, she saw an old box of toys. "Are teddy and ish in there?" she wondered.

"Teddy! Ish! Are you in there?" she called. But they weren't. She did find an old toy mouse, hidden away at the back. "Doesn't anyone love you?" she asked. "You're very soft and cuddly – I'll love you! Come on, Mousey," she giggled. "You come home with me." Puddles was feeling much happier.

But Lulu the kitten wasn't. The mouse was her favourite toy and as Puddles trotted off she began to wail.

"Mummy! Mummy! Come quickly!" she cried.

Hattie, Lulu's mum, appeared through a gap in the fence.

"Puddles has taken my Mousey!" sobbed Lulu.

Puddles didn't hear poor Lulu crying. She was dancing around the garden with her new friend. "Now all I need is an ish," she laughed happily.

As she skipped through the garden next door, Puddles saw a tatty old scarf hanging down from the branch of an apple tree. "Oh look, Mousey!" she cried. "A cuddly ish with no one to love it."

"Well, it's not really an ish," she thought, "but it is very, very soft." She reached up and took one end in her mouth. With a pull and a tug, the scarf floated down; now she was really happy.

She didn't see Lenny, Lulu's brother, fast asleep in the flowerbed. But then Lenny woke up and saw

Puddles skipping off along the garden with his favourite scarf! "Mummy! Mummy!" he wailed, "Puddles has stolen my scarf."

Hattie sighed, now both her twins were crying!

Puddles popped through the hedge and ran straight into – the angry alley cats.

"Oh no!" gulped Puddles. "Someone's in trouble, and I think it's *me*!"

Lulu and Lenny were hiding behind Hattie, who looked very cross. Puddles was suddenly scared and she began to cry.

"H-H-Harvey!" she croaked. "Help me!"

Puddles' wailing woke up Harvey and the gang.

"Is that Puddles I can hear?" said Ruffles. "Yes! Run, Harvey, run! Puddles needs your help!"

"I'm coming Puddles," woofed Harvey.

And off he ran, as fast as he could go…

Harvey burst through the hedge. "OK, guys!" he gasped. "What's all the fuss about?"

The angry alley cats began shouting all at once. There was so much noise that Harvey couldn't hear what anyone was saying.

"QUIET!" he barked. "Now then, Hattie, what is all the noise about?"

"That scallywag sister of yours has stolen my twins' favourite toys," grumbled Hattie.

"Did you, Puddles?" asked Harvey, sternly.

"I thought that no one wanted them," she cried, as she gave back Mousey and the scarf. "Sorry, I

only wanted to love them."

"That's OK, Puddles," smiled the twins. "But you see, we love them – lots and lots."

Hattie looked at Puddles and shook her head; she really was an annoying puppy.

"Puddles, you're such a scamp," smiled Harvey.

"But I was only looking for my teddy and my ish," cried Puddles. "I don't know where they are."

"Oh, but I do!" said Harvey. He scooped them from the skip and gave them back to Puddles with a hug and a kiss. "Now, no more trouble today," he said. "Let's all have a dog nap. OK?"

Puddles hugged her teddy and stroked her ish; she was happy again. "Well," said Puddles, looking at Harvey with a naughty grin, "ish and I will be good, but teddy might not!"

— Big —
TOP

t was a grey day in the higgledy-piggledy, messy alley. Harvey and his gang were fed up!

"What we need is some fun!" yawned Bonnie, "I've got an idea…"

Soon Bonnie and Puddles were jumping on an old mattress. BOINGG! BOINGG! BOINGG! They bounced up and down, up and down.

"*This* is fun!" shrieked Puddles. "I bet I can bounce the highest."

"I'm the *Amazing Bouncing Bonnie*," giggled Bonnie. "Look!"

She bounced high
into the air – and
landed with a thud
on a clump of grass!
"Ooops a daisy,"
she said. "I think I
missed!"

Then Mac clambered onto the washing line.
"WHEEEE! Look! I'm the wibbly wobbly dog."

"Oh no!" gasped Patchy. "Here comes tumble
time," as Mac toppled over onto the mattress
below. Mac sat up and rubbed his head, grinning.

Harvey laughed. His friends' tricks had given
him an idea. "Let's put on a circus," he said.

The Alley Dogs all agreed and they scampered
off to the playground in search of their big top!

"We need to make a circus ring," said Harvey,
when they returned.

"Do you think these old tyres will make good
seats?" asked Ruffles.

"Yes!" said Patchy. "And these old plastic bags can be the curtains!"

The big top was soon ready.

"Well done!" smiled Harvey.

"We must let everyone know that the circus is in town!" said Harvey. "Come on, Ruffles, you've got the loudest voice."

So, Ruffles took a deep breath and boomed out loud, "Roll up! Roll up! Come to Harvey's Big Top. See the Greatest Show on Earth!"

Soon the air was filled with woofing and yapping as their pals queued up to see the circus!

Harvey took a deep breath and stepped into the ring. "And now, ladies and gentlemen," he cried, "please give a big, warm woof for Harvey's Amazing Daring Dogs!"

The audience clapped and stamped their paws!

But the gang did not appear.

"Harvey," Mac called, "we've got the doggy-wobbles!"

Harvey crept behind the curtain. His friends were quivering and quaking. "Silly Billies," he smiled. "There's nothing to be scared of. Watch me."

He quickly pulled on a cape and ran back into the ring.

"Let the show begin with Harvey the Brave!" he cried, and the audience gave a loud cheer.

"For my first trick," he announced, "the Tricky Tightrope!"

He wobbled across the top of the swing from one end to the other – and didn't fall off once.

"How does he do it?" gasped the audience, holding their breath in wonder. "Whatever next?"

Harvey climbed to the top of a big pile of bricks.

"Eeek! What if he falls?" squeaked a little dog. "I can't bear to look."

But Harvey made it – and balanced on one paw!

The Alley Dogs peeped out from behind the curtain. Harvey was having such a good time that it didn't look in the least bit scary. So at last, Harvey's Amazing Daring Dogs rushed to join in with the fun.

"Look at me," said Ruffles. "I can balance a ball on my tummy."

The audience laughed and cheered and clapped.
Patchy and Mac tumbled and turned on their
bouncy mattress – what a pair of acrobats!

The show ended with the daring Trolley Trick.
Bonnie and Ruffles stood on the bottom, Patchy and
Mac climbed onto their shoulders and little Puddles
balanced on the very tip top. When they were ready,
Harvey pushed the trolley round and round the ring.

"More! More!" roared the crowd, as the show
came to an end.

"Well, Puddles," smiled Harvey, when they got
back to their higgledy-piggledy, messy alley, "was
that boring, boring, boring?"

"Oh no, Harvey," she said.
"It wasn't boring, it was
fun, fun, fun!"

—Water—
HUNT

n the higgledy-piggledy, messy alley it was a very hot day. Harvey and his gang were melting!

"I need a slurpy, slippy ice lolly," sighed Ruffles.

"I need a cool pool to roll in," squeaked Puddles.

Those hot dogs just didn't know what to do!

"It's too hot to sleep," complained Bonnie. "I'm the hottest dog in the world!"

"No, I'm hotter than you!" snorted Ruffles.

"Oh no, you're not," replied Patchy, grumpily. "I *know* I am!"

"I haven't been this hot," said Mac, "since I was in the desert when—"

"*Not now, Mac!*" the other dogs all yelled at once.

"We're too hot to do anything," said Patchy.

"Except nosh yummy ice cold ice cream," replied Ruffles, with a grin.

"I know," cried Mac suddenly. "Let's go to the seaside! We could play in the sand and splish and splash in the water."

"Good thinking, Mac," smiled Harvey. "But it's too far for us to go on a day like today. Can you think of something else?"

"Let's all go to the park," suggested Patchy. "We could jump in and out of the paddling pool and play in the fountain."

Poor Puddles looked as though she were going to burst into tears.

"I can't walk that far, Harvey," she whispered. "I've only got little legs!"

"Don't worry, Puddles," said Harvey kindly. "We wouldn't go without you."

"Oh, there must be some water somewhere!" puffed and panted Patchy.

"If I don't find water soon, I'm going to melt into a big, hairy puddle!" groaned Ruffles.

Those poor hot dogs – what could they do?

Meanwhile, the sizzling Alley Cats were searching, too. But they weren't on a water hunt. Oh no! They were on a mouse hunt – Archie had lost his favourite toy mouse!

"I WANT IT BACK!" wailed Archie, looking under a box.

"Well, it's not in here!" called Bertie from the top of a flower pot.

"Phew!" groaned Hattie. "It's way too hot for hunting, Archie. Why don't we have a catnap instead?"

"Catnap time!" said Lucy. "Great idea."

So the Alley Cats snuggled down for an afternoon nap – or did they?

Lenny and Lulu – the two little kittens – weren't quite ready for a nap yet!

"Naps are for babies," whispered Lenny to his sister. "Come on, Lulu, follow me."

"Yippee!" giggled Lulu. "An adventure."

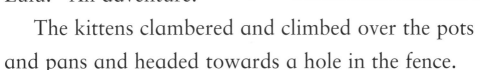

The kittens clambered and climbed over the pots and pans and headed towards a hole in the fence.

"Hey, Lulu!" cried Lenny. "I bet we find Archie's mouse through here."

So, carefully and quietly, the kittens squeezed themselves through the tiny gap—

Suddenly, a strange, stripy monster jumped out in front of them!

"AAAAAGH!" screamed Lulu. "What is it?"

Swooping and swaying through the spiky grass, it wiggled towards them, and then lifted up its head and gave a loud, angry "HISSSSS!"

"It's a snake!" yelled Lenny. "Let's scarper."

Running as fast as they could, the kittens bounded towards a tree trunk and scampered up into its branches!

Lenny and Lulu quivered and quaked.

"HELP!" they wailed.

As the snake swayed about in front of the kittens, the poor little pussies began to cry.

With one, last enormous "HISSSSSSS!", the swinging snake leapt towards them – and got stuck in a branch!

Suddenly a great big spurt of water gushed from the snake's mouth, shot over the fence and into the alley below – SPLOOOSH!

Those silly scallywags. It wasn't a snake at all. It was a hosepipe and the cool refreshing water woke up Harvey and the gang – they couldn't believe their eyes!

"It's rainy and sunny at the same time," laughed Harvey.

He looked up and saw Lenny and Lulu peeping shyly over the fence.

"You clever cats," he called up to them.

"Three cheers for Lenny and Lulu!" cried Harvey.

And so, two cool cats had made five hot dogs very happy!

—Little Red— RIDING —Hood—

Once upon a time there was a little girl who lived with her mother at the edge of a deep, dark forest. Everyone called the girl Little Red Riding Hood, because she always wore a bright red cloak with a bright red hood.

One sunny morning her mother said, "Granny isn't feeling very well. Please will you take this basket of goodies to her, to make her feel better?"

"I will," replied Little Red Riding Hood.

"Remember," said her mother, "stay on the path, and don't stop to talk to any strangers on the way."

Little Red Riding Hood hopped and skipped along the path to Granny's house. She had only gone a short way into the deep, dark forest, when a sly, nasty wolf with big shiny teeth and long sharp claws jumped out onto the path, right in front of her.

"Hello, my pretty one," said the wolf. "Where are you going on this fine morning?"

"Good morning," said Little Red Riding Hood politely. "I'm going to see my granny, who isn't feeling very well. She lives all the way on the other side of the forest. But please excuse me, I am not allowed to talk to strangers."

"Of course little girl," sneered the crafty wolf. "Why not take a moment to pick a big bunch of these lovely wild flowers to cheer your granny up?"

"Thank you, Mr Wolf, that's a very good idea," said Little Red Riding Hood.

So, while Little Red Riding Hood picked a bunch of sweet-smelling flowers, the wicked wolf raced ahead through the deep, dark forest and soon arrived at Granny's pretty cottage. The wolf lifted the knocker and banged hard at the door. Sweet old Granny sat up in bed. "Who is it?" she called.

"It's me, Little Red Riding Hood," replied the wolf in a voice just like Little Red Riding Hood's.

"Hello, my dear," called Granny. "The door is not locked – lift up the latch and come in."

So the wolf opened
the door and, quick as
a flash, he gobbled
Granny up. Then he
put on her nightie and
nightcap, and crawled
under the bedcovers to
lie in wait for Little
Red Riding Hood.

A while later, Little Red Riding Hood arrived at
the cottage and knocked on Granny's door.

"Who is it?" called the wolf, in a voice just like
Granny's.

"It's me, Granny," replied Little Red Riding Hood.

"Hello, my dear," called the wolf. "The door is
not locked – lift up the latch and come in."

So Little Red Riding Hood lifted the latch,
opened the door and went into Granny's cottage.

Little Red Riding Hood couldn't believe her eyes.
"Oh, Granny," she said, "it is so nice to see you,

but what big ears you have!"

"All the better to hear you with," said the wolf.

"Oh, Granny," she said, "what big eyes you have!"

"All the better to see you with," said the wolf. "Come closer, my dear."

So Little Red Riding Hood took another step closer. Now she was right beside Granny's bed.

"Granny!" she cried. "What big teeth you have!"

"All the better to eat you with, my dear!" snarled the wolf, and he jumped up and swallowed Little Red Riding Hood in one BIG gulp!

Now it just so happened that a woodcutter was passing Granny's cottage that morning. He knew that Granny had not been very well, so he decided to visit her. What a surprise he had when he saw the hairy wolf fast asleep in Granny's bed!

When he saw the wolf's big, fat tummy, he knew just what had happened. Quick as a flash, he took out his shiny sharp axe and sliced the wolf open! Out popped Granny and Little Red Riding Hood, surprised and shaken, but safe and well.

The woodcutter dragged the wolf outside and threw him down a deep, dark well so he would never trouble anyone ever again. Then he, Granny and Little Red Riding Hood ate all of the yummy goodies from Little Red Riding Hood's basket.

After tea, Little Red Riding Hood waved goodbye to her Granny and the woodcutter and ran all the way home to her mother, without straying once from the path or talking to any strangers. What an eventful day!

Goldilocks and THE THREE —Bears—

Once upon a time, deep in a dark green forest, there lived a family of bears. There was great big Daddy Bear. There was middle-sized Mummy Bear. And there was little Baby Bear.

One sunny morning, the bears were up early, hungry for their breakfast. Daddy Bear cooked three bowls of porridge. He made it with lots of golden, runny honey, just the way bears like it. "Breakfast is ready!" called Daddy Bear.

But when he poured it into the bowls, it was far too hot to eat!

"We'll just have to let our porridge cool down for a while before we eat it," said Mummy Bear.

"But I'm hungry!" wailed Baby Bear.

"I know, let's go for a walk in the forest while we wait," suggested Mummy Bear. "Get the basket, Baby Bear. We can gather wild berries as we go."

So, leaving the steaming bowls of porridge on the table, the three bears went out into the forest. The last one out was little Baby Bear, and he forgot to close the front door behind him.

The sun was shining brightly through the trees that morning and someone else was walking in the forest. It was a little girl called Goldilocks, who had long, curly golden hair and the cutest nose you ever did see.

Goldilocks was skipping happily through the forest when suddenly she smelt something yummy and delicious – whatever could it be?

She followed the smell until she came to the three bears' cottage. It seemed to be coming from inside. The door was open, so she peeped in and saw three bowls of porridge on the table.

Goldilocks just couldn't resist the lovely sweet smell. So, even though she knew she shouldn't go into anyone's house without first being invited, she tiptoed inside.

First, she tasted the porridge in Daddy Bear's great big bowl, but it was too hot. So she tried Mummy Bear's middle-sized bowl, but it was too sweet. Finally, she tried the porridge in

Baby Bear's tiny little bowl. "Yummy!" This porridge is just right!" So Goldilocks ate it all up – every last drop!

Then Goldilocks decided she wanted to sit down. First, she sat in Daddy Bear's great big chair, but it was too hard. So she tried Mummy Bear's middle-sized chair, but it was too soft. Finally, Goldilocks tried Baby Bear's tiny little chair – and it was just right!

But as Goldilocks settled down, it broke into lots of little pieces! Goldilocks picked herself up off the floor and looked for a place to lie down.

First, Goldilocks tried Daddy Bear's great big bed, but it was too hard. So she tried Mummy Bear's middle-sized bed but it was far too soft. Finally, she tried Baby Bear's tiny little bed and it was just right! So Goldilocks climbed in, pulled the blanket up to her chin and fell fast, fast asleep.

Not long after, the three bears came home from their walk, ready for their yummy porridge.

"Someone's been eating my porridge!" said Daddy and Mummy Bear, together.

"Someone's been eating my porridge," cried Baby Bear. "And they've eaten it all up!"

Then Daddy Bear said, "Look, Mummy Bear! Someone's been sitting in my chair!"

And Mummy Bear said, "Look, Daddy Bear! Someone's been sitting in *my* chair."

"Someone's been sitting in *my* chair, too," cried Baby Bear. "And look! They've broken it all to pieces!" They all stared at the bits of broken chair. Then Baby Bear burst into tears.

Suddenly, the three bears heard the tiniest of noises. Was it a creak? Was it a groan? No, it was a snore, and it came from their bedroom.

They crept up the stairs very, quietly…

"Someone's been sleeping in my bed!" cried Daddy Bear.

"Someone's been sleeping in my bed," said Mummy Bear.

"Someone's been sleeping in my bed!" cried Baby Bear. "And look, she's still there!"

All this noise woke Goldilocks up with a start.

When she saw the three bears standing over her, Goldilocks was very scared. "Oh, dear! Oh, dear! Oh, dear!" she cried, jumping out of Baby Bear's bed. She ran out of the bedroom, down the stairs, out of the front door and all the way back home – and she never ever came back to the forest again!

—Sleeping—
BEAUTY

Once upon a time, in a land far, far away, there lived a king and queen who were kind and good. When the queen gave birth to a baby girl, the whole kingdom rejoiced.

When it was time for the baby to be christened, the king and queen arranged a great celebration. They asked the seven good fairies of the kingdom to be the baby's godmothers. But eight fairies arrived at the feast.

The eighth fairy was ugly and old, and no one had seen

her for years. The king and queen, thinking she was dead, hadn't invited her to the ceremony.

Soon it was time for the fairies to give the baby princess their magical presents. The first gave the gift of beauty, the second gave wisdom. The third fairy gave grace, the fourth said that she would dance like the wind. The fifth and sixth gave her the gift of music and song.

Then the eighth fairy pushed ahead of the seventh fairy. "The princess will prick her finger on the spindle of a spinning wheel – and die!" she cackled.

Everyone in the room was horrified. But then the seventh fairy stepped forward.

"Here is my gift," she said. "When she pricks her finger, the princess will fall asleep for a hundred years. Then, a prince will come to wake her up."

The king and queen were relieved, but even so they ordered every spinning wheel in the kingdom to be destroyed.

The years passed and the princess grew into a lovely young girl, as wise, beautiful and graceful as the fairies had promised. On the day of her sixteenth birthday, she was wandering through the castle when she came to a small room in a tall

tower. Inside, an old woman sat spinning thread.

"My dear," cackled the old woman, "come and try this."

As soon as the princess's hand touched the spindle, she pricked her finger and fell to the floor in a deep sleep.

When they found their daughter, the king and queen were heartbroken, for they knew that she would not wake for a hundred years. They called for the palace guard, who gently laid the sleeping princess on a golden

stretcher and carried her to the royal bedchamber.

The fairy who had saved the princess's life heard what had happened. Worried that the princess would wake up in a world where she knew no one, she cast a spell over the whole castle. Everyone – even the princess's pet dog – fell into a deep sleep.

Then the fairy made trees and sharp brambles grow around the castle, surrounding it with a thick wall that no one could get through. Only the very tops of the castle's towers could be seen.

And so a hundred years went by.

One day, a prince was out riding when he saw the tops of the castle towers. He asked the villagers about it, and they told him about Sleeping Beauty.

"Many people have wanted to get through those thorns," they told him, "but they have died trying."

The prince set off towards the mysterious castle, and strangely the thorny brambles and the twisting branches of the dark trees let him pass through.

The prince ran through halls and chambers where people and animals slept as if they were dead. He searched every room and chamber, until he found where the beautiful princess slept.

"Oh, princess!" cried the prince. "You are more

beautiful than the most
delicate rose ever found."

The prince gazed
down lovingly at her.
He gently took her tiny
hand in his, and knelt
beside her and kissed her
red lips. Instantly the
princess's eyes opened.

"Is it you, my prince?"
she said, when she saw
him. "I have waited such a long time for you!"

At that moment the spell was broken, and
everyone else in the castle woke up, too.

That evening, the princess's sixteenth birthday
was celebrated with a joyous party – just a hundred
years too late!

The princess and her prince danced together all
evening, and soon after, were married. They lived
together in happiness for many, many years.

CINDERELLA

Once upon a time, there lived a pretty little girl. When she was young, her mother sadly died. Her father remarried, but the girl's stepmother was a mean woman with two ugly daughters. These

stepsisters were so jealous of the young girl's beauty that they treated her like a servant and made her sit in the cinders in the kitchen.

They called her Cinderella, and before long even her father had forgotten her real name.

One day, an invitation arrived from the royal palace. The king and queen were holding a ball for the prince's twenty-first birthday, and all the fine ladies of the kingdom were invited.

Cinderella's stepsisters were very excited. "I will wear my red velvet gown!" cried the first stepsister. "And the pearl necklace that Mother gave to me."

"And I will wear my blue silk dress!" cried the other. "With a silver tiara."

"Come, Cinderella!" they called. "You must help us to get ready!"

Cinderella helped her stepsisters with their silk stockings and frilly petticoats. She brushed and curled their hair and powdered their cheeks and noses. At last, she squeezed them into their beautiful ball gowns.

Cinderella said nothing, but inside, her heart was breaking. She really wanted to go to the ball. After her stepsisters left, she sat and wept.

"Dry your tears, my dear," said a gentle voice.

Cinderella was amazed. An old woman stood before her, with a sparkly wand in her hand.

"I am your Fairy Godmother," she said. "And you shall go to the ball!"

The Fairy Godmother asked Cinders to fetch her the biggest pumpkin in the garden. With a flick of her magic wand she turned it into a golden carriage

and the mice in the kitchen mousetrap into fine horses. A fat rat soon became a handsome coachman.

Smiling at Cinderella's surprised face, the Fairy Godmother waved her wand once more. Cinderella was dressed in a splendid ball-gown. On her feet were sparkling glass slippers.

"My magic will end at midnight, so you must be home before then," said the Fairy Godmother. "Good luck."

Everyone was dazzled by her beauty. Whispers and gasps sounded round the ballroom as the other guests wondered who this stranger could be. Even Cinderella's own stepsisters did not recognise her.

As soon as the prince set eyes on Cinderella, he fell in love with her, and asked her to dance with him.

"Why certainly, sir," Cinderella answered. And from that moment on he only had eyes for Cinderella.

Soon the clock struck midnight. "I must go!" said Cinderella, remembering her promise. She fled from the ballroom and ran down the palace steps. The prince ran after her, but when he got

outside, she was gone. He didn't notice a grubby servant girl holding a pumpkin. A few mice and a rat scurried around her feet. But there on the steps was one dainty glass slipper.

The next day, the stepsisters could only talk of the ball, and the beautiful stranger who had danced all night with the prince. As they were talking, there was a knock at the door.

On the doorstep was His Highness the Prince and a royal footman, who was holding the little glass

slipper on a velvet cushion.

"The lady whose foot this slipper fits is my one and only true love," said the prince.

The two stepsisters began shoving each other out of the way in their rush to try on the slipper.

They both squeezed and pushed, but their clumsy feet were far too big for the tiny glass shoe.

Then Cinderella stepped forward. "Please, Your Highness," she said, shyly, "may I try?"

Cinderella's foot slid into the dainty shoe, which fitted as if it were made for her! As the prince gazed into her eyes, he knew he had found his love – and Cinderella knew she had found hers.

On the day of their wedding, the land rang to the sound of bells, and the sun shone as the people smiled and cheered. Even Cinderella's nasty stepsisters were invited.
Everyone had
a really
wonderful
day, and
Cinderella
and her prince
lived happily
ever after.

Jack and the BEANSTALK

Jack was a lively young boy who lived with his mother in a tiny little cottage in the country. Jack and his mother were very poor. They had straw on the floor, and many panes of glass in their windows were broken. The only thing of value that was left was a cow.

One day, Jack's mother called him in from the garden, where he was chopping logs for their stove. "You will have to take Daisy the cow to market and sell her," she said sadly.

As Jack trudged along the long road to market, he met a strange old man.

"Where are you taking that fine milking cow?" asked the man.

"To market, sir," replied Jack, "to sell her."

"If you sell her to me," said the man, "I will give you these beans. They are special, magic beans."

When Jack heard the word "magic", he became very excited. He quickly swapped the cow for the beans, and ran home.

"Why are you home so soon?" asked Jack's mother. "How much did you get for the cow?"

"I got these magic beans!" said Jack

"What?" shrieked his mother. "A handful of beans? You silly boy!"

Angrily, she snatched the beans from Jack's hand and flung them out of the window, into the garden. Jack was sent to bed with no supper that night.

The next morning, Jack's rumbling stomach woke him early. As he got dressed, he glanced out of his window – and what he saw took his breath away.

Overnight, a beanstalk had sprung up in the garden. Its trunk was as thick as Jack's cottage and

its top was so tall that it disappeared into the clouds. Jack yelled with excitement, rushed outside and began to climb the trunk.

At last Jack reached the top and found himself in a strange land full of clouds.

Jack walked until he

came to the biggest castle he had ever seen. He crept under the front door – straight into a huge foot!

"Who are you?" boomed a female voice, and the whole room shook. Suddenly, he was whisked into the air by a giant hand!

"I'm Jack," said Jack, "and I'm tired and hungry. Please can you give me something to eat and a place to rest for a while?"

"Be quiet!" said the giantess. "My husband will eat you if he finds you." Then she gave Jack a crumb of warm bread and a thimble full of hot soup.

He was just finishing the last drop when the giant's wife said, "Quick! Hide in the cupboard! My husband's coming!"

Jack heard a deep voice bellow, "Fee, fie, foe, fum, I smell the blood of an Englishman! Be he alive or be he dead, I'll grind his bones to make my bread!"

Jack peeped out through a hole in the cupboard door, and saw a giant standing beside the table.

"Wife!" shouted the giant. "I can smell a boy!"

"Nonsense, dear," said the giant's wife. "All you can smell is this lovely dinner I have made for you."

When the giant had gobbled up his dinner and a huge bowl of pudding, he shouted, "Wife! Bring me my gold! I wish to count it!"

The giant's wife brought several big sacks and

Jack watched as the giant counted his gold coins. Soon he was yawning, and then he was snoring, loudly!

Quick as a flash, Jack leapt onto the table, grabbed a sack of gold, and ran for the door as fast as he could.

The giant's wife screamed, "Stop, thief!" at the top of her voice. This woke her husband who ran after Jack, shouting loudly, "Come back!"

Jack ran to the top of the beanstalk and then scrambled down as fast as he could.

"Mother!" he called, as he got closer to the ground. "Mother, get the axe, quickly!"

By the time Jack reached the bottom, his mother chopped down the beanstalk, and the giant came crashing down with it – he never got up again!

Now that they had the gold, Jack and his mother were very rich. They would never have to worry about anything ever again and they both lived happily ever after.

Written by Gaby Goldsack and
Jan and Tony Payne (Likely Stories)
Illustrated by Alison Atkins, Martin Grant (Advocate),
Daniel Howarth (Advocate), Paula Martyr, Peter
Rutherford and Rory Tyger (Advocate)
Language consultant: Betty Root

This is a Parragon Book
This edition published in 2004

Parragon
Queen Street House
4 Queen Street
Bath BA1 1HE, UK

Copyright © Parragon 2003

Printed in China

ISBN 1-40544-159-3